A NOMAD OF THE TIME STREAMS NOVEL

THE SECOND ADVENTURE
THE LAND LEVIATHAN

A NOMAD OF THE TIME STREAMS NOVEL

THE SECOND ADVENTURE

THE LAND LEVIATHAN

A NEW SCIENTIFIC ROMANCE

MICHAEL MOORCOCK

TITAN BOOKS

The Land Leviathan
Print edition ISBN: 9781781161463
E-book edition ISBN: 9781781161494

Published by Titan Books
A division of Titan Publishing Group Ltd
144 Southwark Street, London SE1 0UP

First edition: April 2013
1 3 5 7 9 10 8 6 4 2

Edited by John Davey.

A CIP catalogue record for this title is available from the British Library.

Printed and bound in the United States.

Did you enjoy this book? We love to hear from our readers.
Please email us at readerfeedback@titanemail.com or write to us at
Reader Feedback at the above address.

To receive advance information, news, competitions, and exclusive offers online,
please sign up for the Titan newsletter on our website: www.titanbooks.com

To the Memory of
Steve Biko, Malcolm X, and Mongezi Feza

FOREWORD

First published between 1971 and 1981, Michael Moorcock's *The Warlord of the Air* (or is it *The War Lord of the Air?*—editions vary), *The Land Leviathan* and *The Steel Tsar*—three books known collectively as "The Oswald Bastable Trilogy" or "A Nomad of the Time Streams"—look backwards, forwards and sideways at the same time.

In 1969, there were people going around seriously saying that science fiction would die as a genre after the moon landing. The future was here, so we didn't need to think about it any more. Certainly, the genre had been around long enough by then for its earlier examples to seem comically outdated—all those books and stories where there's a breathable atmosphere on the moon, or astro-navigators fiddle with slide rules on their faster-than-light spaceships. Still, there were people who saw the beauty and the terror and (most importantly) the continued relevance of the futures which didn't happen.

In Moorcock's novels, army officer Oswald Bastable—the name comes from a series of books by E. Nesbit, author of *Five Children and It*—comes unstuck in time from his own era (1903) and tours three overlapping, yet different, imagined versions of the twentieth century… where the British Empire persists into the 1970s, technological advances lead to a war that leaves the world in ruins in the early 1900s and a Russian revolution did not lead to a Soviet state. Constant in all these fractured mirrors of our own history are airships, stately hold-overs from the exciting books of Jules Verne (*The Clipper of the Clouds*) and George Griffith (*The Angel of the Revolution*), and the atomic bomb (which arrived in fiction in 1914 in H.G. Wells' *The World Set Free*). The point is not, as in some meticulously constructed and argued alternative histories, to imagine how things might have been, but to confront the way things really were, as our collective urges for incompatible utopias brought about horrors beyond imagining. Though not averse to blaming individuals, these books are strong on collective responsibility: there are versions here of Joseph Stalin, Ronald Reagan, Enoch Powell and Harold Wilson, as sad little men whose small-minded blind spots, ambitions and cruelties bring about personal and global disasters. But no one is let off the hook, and we're all to blame.

The voice of these novels is a perfect match for the Victorian and Edwardian authors evoked over and over in them… not just Wells, Nesbit and Griffith, but Rider Haggard, Conan Doyle, Rudyard Kipling (*With the Night Mail*), Saki (*When William Came*—a novel Moorcock brought back into print in the anthology *England Invaded*), George Tomkyns Chesney (*The Battle of Dorking*) and many other scientific romancers of the nineteenth and early twentieth centuries. Moorcock can embrace, with love, the idealism and imagination expressed in these writers' works, though as many were catastrophists as utopians, but recognises that they share in the collective responsibility for the way the world really turned out. A key influence on the steampunk movement in contemporary fantasy, these books are spikier, more clear-sighted and complicated than most superficially similar visions of technological Victoriana.

These books are Griffith-like yarns—full of scrapes, adventures, exotica, jokes, plot reversals and charm—but they're at heart serious, sobering visions. I am delighted they are available again, and so will you be.

KIM NEWMAN
London, 2012

f

INTRODUCTION

My grandfather, who died relatively young after he had volunteered for service in the Great War, became increasingly secretive and misanthropic in his last years so that the discovery of a small steel safe amongst his effects was unsurprising and aroused no curiosity whatsoever in his heirs who, finding that they could not unlock it (no key ever came to light), simply stored it away with his papers and forgot about it. The safe remained in the attic of our Yorkshire house for the best part of fifty years and doubtless would still be there if it had not been for my discovery of the manuscript which I published a couple of years ago under the title *The Warlord of the Air*. After the book was published I received many interesting letters from people asking me if it was merely a piece of fiction or if the story had come into my hands as I had described. I, of course, believed Bastable's story (and my grandfather's) completely, yet sometimes felt quite as frustrated as my grandfather had done when he had tried to get people to share *his* belief, and I couldn't help brooding occasionally on the mystery of the young man's disappearance after those long hours spent talking to my grandfather on Rowe Island in the early years of the century.

As it turned out, I was soon to find myself in possession of, for me, the best possible proof of my grandfather's veracity, if not of Bastable's.

I spent this past summer in Yorkshire, where we have a house overlooking the moors of the West Riding, and, having little to do but go for long walks and enjoy the pleasures of rock climbing, I took to looking through the rest of my grandfather's things, coming at length upon the old steel safe jammed in a corner under the eaves of one of our innumerable attics. The safe was hidden behind the moulting remains of a stuffed timber wolf which had used to terrify me as a child, and perhaps that was the reason why I had not previously found it. As I pushed the beast aside, his dusty glass eyes seemed to glare at me with hurt dignity and he toppled slowly sideways and fell with a muffled crash into a heap of yellowing newspapers which another of my relatives, for reasons of his own, had once thought worth preserving. It was as if the wolf had been guarding the safe since the beginning of Time, and I had a slight feeling of invading hallowed ground, much as some booty-hunting Victorian archaeologist must have felt as he chipped his way into the tomb of a dead Egyptian king!

The safe was about eighteen inches deep and a couple of feet high, made of thick steel. The outside had grown a little rusty and the handle would not budge when I tried it. I hunted about the house for spare keys which might fit the lock, finding the best part of a score of keys, but none which would open the safe. By now my curiosity was fully whetted and I manhandled the safe downstairs and took it into my workshop where I tried to force it. All I succeeded in doing was to break two or three chisels and ruin the blades of my hacksaw, so eventually I had to telephone a specialist locksmith in Leeds and ask for expert help in opening the thing. I was pessimistically certain that the safe would contain only some out-of-date share certificates or nothing at all, but I knew I should not be able to rest until it *was* opened. The locksmith came, eventually, and it took him only a short while to get the safe undone.

I remember the rather sardonic look he offered me as the contents were displayed for the first time in almost sixty years. It was plain that he thought I had wasted my money, for there were no family treasures here, merely a pile of closely written foolscap sheets, beginning to show their age. The handwriting was not even my grandfather's and I experienced a distinct sinking sensation, for obviously I had hoped to find notes which would tell me more about Bastable and my grandfather's experiences after he had set off for China to seek the Valley of the Morning, where he had guessed Bastable to be.

As he left, the locksmith gave me what I guessed to be a pitying look and said that his firm would be sending the bill along later. I sighed, made myself a pot of coffee, and then sat down to leaf through the sheets.

Only then did I realize that I had found something even more revealing than anything I had hoped to discover (and, it emerged, even more mystifying!)—*for these notes were Bastable's own.* Here, written in his hand, was an account of his experiences after he had left my grandfather—there was even a brief note addressed to him from Bastable:

Moorcock. I hope this reaches you. Make of it what you will. I'm going to try my luck again. This time if I am not successful I doubt I shall have the courage to continue with my life (if it *is* mine).

Yours—Bastable

Attached to this were some sheets in my grandfather's flowing handwriting and these I reproduce in the body of the text, making it the first section.

This first section is self-explanatory. There is little I need to add at all. You may read the rest for yourself and make up your own mind as to its authenticity.

MICHAEL MOORCOCK

Ladbroke Grove

London

January 1971

PROLOGUE

In Search of Oswald Bastable

If I were ever to write a book of travel, no matter how queer the events it described, I am sure I would never have the same trouble placing it with a publisher as I had when I tried to get into print Oswald Bastable's strange tale of his visit to the future in the year 1973. People are not alarmed by the unusual so long as it is placed in an acceptable context. A book describing as fact the discovery of a race of four-legged, three-eyed men of abnormal intelligence and supernatural powers who live in Thibet would probably be taken by a large proportion of the public as absolutely credible. Similarly, if I had dressed up Bastable's story as fiction I am certain that critics would have praised me for my rich imagination and that a reasonably wide audience would have perused it in a couple of summer afternoons and thought it a jolly exciting read for the money, then promptly forgotten all about it.

Perhaps it is what I should have done, but, doubtless irrationally, I felt that I had a duty to Bastable to publish his account as it stood.

I could, were I trying to make money with my pen, write

a whole book, full of sensational anecdotes, concerning my travels in China—a country divided by both internal and external pressures, where the only real law can be found in the territories leased to various foreign powers, and where a whole variety of revolutionists and prophets of peculiar political and religious sects squabble continuously for a larger share of that vast and ancient country; but my object is not to make money from Bastable's story. I merely think it is up to me to keep my word to him and do my best to put it before the public.

Now that I have returned home, with some relief, to England, I have become a little more optimistic about China's chances of saving herself from chaos and foreign exploitation. There has been the revolution resulting in the deposing of the last of the Manchus and the setting up of a republic under Sun Yat-sen, who seems to be a reasonable and moderate leader, a man who has learned a great deal from the political history of Europe and yet does not seem content just to ape the customs of the West. Possibly there is hope for China now. However, it is not my business here to speculate upon China's political future, but to record how I traveled to the Valley of the Morning, following Bastable's somewhat vague description of its location. I had gathered that it lay somewhere in Shantung province and to the north of Wuchang (which, itself, of course, is in Hupeh). My best plan was to go as directly as possible to Shantung and then make my way inland. I consulted all the atlases and gazetteers, spoke to friends who had been missionaries in that part of China, and got a fairly clear idea of where I might find the valley, if it existed at all.

Yet I was still reluctant to embark upon what was likely to be a long and exhausting expedition. For all that I had completely believed Bastable, I had no evidence at all to substantiate my theory that he had gone back to the Valley of the Morning, which, by 1973, would contain the Utopian city built by General Shaw, the Warlord of the Air, and called Chi'ng Che'eng Ta-Chia (or, in

English, roughly Democratic Dawn City). Even if he had gone there—and found nothing—he could easily have disappeared into the vastness of the Asian continent and as easily have perished in one of the minor wars or uprisings which constantly ravaged those poor and strife-ridden lands.

Therefore I continued to lead my conventional life, putting the whole perplexing business of Captain Bastable as far into the back of my mind as possible, although I would patiently send his original manuscript to a fresh publisher every time it came back from the last. I also sent a couple of letters to *The Times* in the hope that my story of my meeting with Bastable would attract the attention of that or some other newspaper, but the letters were never published. Neither, it seemed, were any of the popular monthlies, like the *Strand*, interested, for all that their pages were full of wild and unlikely predictions of what the future was bound to hold for us. I even considered writing to Mr. H.G. Wells, whose books *Anticipations* and *The Discovery of the Future* created such a stir a few years ago, but Mr. Wells, whom I understood to be a full-blooded socialist, would probably have found Bastable's story too much out of sympathy with his views and would have ignored me as cheerfully as anyone else. I did draft a letter, but finally did not send it.

It was about this time that it was brought to my attention that I was beginning to earn a reputation as something of a crank. This was a reputation I felt I could ill afford and it meant that I was forced, at last, to come to a decision. I had been noticing, for several months, a slightly odd atmosphere at my London club. People I had known for years, albeit only acquaintances, seemed reluctant to pass the time of day with me, and others would sometimes direct looks at me which were downright cryptic. I was not particularly bothered by any of this, but the mystery, such as it was, was finally made clear to me by an old friend of mine who was, himself, a publisher, although he concentrated entirely on poetry and novels and so I had never had occasion to submit Bastable's manuscript to him. He knew of it, however, and had initially been able to give me the names of one or two publishers who might have been interested. Now, however, he approached me in the library of the club where, after lunch, I had gone to read for half-an-hour. He attracted my attention with a discreet cough.

"Hope you don't mind me interrupting, Moorcock."

"Not at all." I indicated a nearby chair. "As a matter of fact I wanted a word with you, old boy. I'm still having trouble placing that manuscript I mentioned…"

He ignored my offer of a chair and remained standing.

"That's exactly what I wanted to talk to you about. I've been meaning to speak to you for a month or two now, but to tell you the truth I've had no idea how to approach you. This must sound like damned interference and I'd be more than grateful if you would take what I have to say in the spirit it's meant."

He looked extraordinarily embarrassed, squirming like a schoolboy. I even thought I detected the trace of a blush on his cheeks.

I laughed.

"You're making me extremely curious, old man. What is it?"

"You won't be angry—no—you've every reason to be angry. It's not that I believe—"

"Come on, out with it." I put my book down and gave him a smile. "We're old friends, you and I."

"Well, Moorcock, it's *about* Bastable's manuscript. A lot of people—mainly in publishing, of course, but quite a few of them are members of the club—well, they think you've been duped by the chap who told you that story."

"Duped?" I raised my eyebrows.

He looked miserably at the carpet. "Or worse," he murmured.

"I think you'd better tell me what they're saying." I frowned. "I'm sure you mean well and I assure you that I'll take anything you have to say in good part. I've known you too long to be offended."

He was plainly relieved and came and sat down in the next chair. "Well," he began, "most people think that you're the victim of a hoax. But a few are beginning to believe that you've turned a bit—a bit eccentric. Like those chaps who predict the end of the world all the time, or communicate with the astral plane, and so on. You know what I mean, I suppose."

My answering smile must have seemed to him a bit grim. "I know exactly what you mean. I had even considered it. It must seem a very rum go to someone who never met Bastable. Now you mention it, I'm not surprised if I'm the gossip of half London. Why shouldn't people think such things about me? I'd be tempted to think them myself about *you* if you came to me with a story like Bastable's. As it is, you've been extremely tolerant of me!"

His smile was weak as he tried to acknowledge my joke. I went on:

"So they think I'm a candidate for Colney Hatch, do they? Well, of course, I've absolutely no proof to the contrary. If only I could produce Bastable himself. Then people could make up their own minds about the business."

"It *has* become something of an obsession," suggested my friend gently. "Perhaps it would be better to drop the whole thing?"

"You're right—it is an obsession. I happen to believe that Bastable was telling the truth."

"That's as may be…"

"You mean I should stop my efforts to get the account into print."

There was a hint of sorrow in his eyes. "There isn't a publisher in London, old man, who would touch it now. They have *their* reputations to think of. Anyone who took it would be a laughing-stock. That's why you've had so much trouble in placing it. Drop it, Moorcock, for your sake and everyone else's."

"You could be right." I sighed. "Yet, if I could come up with some sort of proof, possibly then they would stop laughing."

"How could you find the proof which would convince them?"

"I could go and look for Bastable in China and tell him the trouble he's caused me. I could hope that he would come back to London with me—talk to people himself. I could put the matter into his hands and let him deal with his own manuscript. What would you say to that?"

He shrugged and made a gesture with his right hand. "I agree it would be better than nothing."

"But your own opinion is that I should forget all about it. You think I should burn the manuscript and have done with it, once and for all?"

"That's my opinion, yes. For your own sake, Moorcock— and your family's. You're wasting so much of your time—not to mention your capital."

"I know that you have my interests at heart," I told him, "but I made a promise to Bastable (although he never heard me make it) and I intend to keep it, if I can. However, I'm glad that you spoke to me. It took courage to do that and I appreciate that it was done with the best of intentions. I'll think the whole thing over, at any rate."

"Yes," he said eagerly, "do think it over. No point in fighting a losing battle, eh? You took this very decently, Moorcock. I was afraid you'd chuck me out on my ear. You had every right to do so."

Again I laughed. "I'm not that much of a lunatic, as you can see. I haven't lost all my common sense. But doubtless anyone with common sense would listen to me and become convinced that I *was* a lunatic! Whether, however, *I* have enough common sense to put the whole obsession behind me is quite another matter!"

He got up. "Let's stop talking about it. Can I buy you a drink?"

For the moment it was obviously politic to accept his offer so that he should not think I had, after all, taken offense. "I'd be glad of one," I said. "I hope the other members aren't afraid that I'm about to run riot with a meat-axe or something!"

As we left the library he clapped me on the shoulder, speaking with some relief. "I don't think so. Though there was some talk of chaining down the soda siphon a week or two ago."

I only went back to the club once more during that period and it was noticeable how much better the atmosphere had become. I determined, there and then, to give up all immediate attempts to get Bastable's story published and I began to make concrete plans for a trip to China.

And so, one bright autumn morning, I arrived at the offices of the Peninsular & Oriental Steam Navigation Company and booked the earliest possible passage on a ship called the *Mother Gangá*, which, I gathered, was not the proudest ship of that particular line, but would be the first to call at Weihaiwei, a city lying on the coast of that part of Shantung leased to Britain in 1898. I thought it only sense to begin my journey in relatively friendly country where I could seek detailed advice and help before pressing on into the interior.

Mother Gangá took her time. She was an old ship and she had evidently come to the conclusion that nothing in the world was urgent enough to require her to hurry. She called at every possible port to unload one cargo and to load another, for she was not primarily a passenger ship at all. It was easy to see why she rid herself of some of her cargoes (which seemed completely worthless), but hard to understand why the traders in those small, obscure ports should be prepared to exchange something of relative value for them!

I was prepared for the slowness of the journey, however, and spent much of my time working out the details of my plans and poring over my original shorthand notes to see if Bastable had told me anything more which might offer a clue to his whereabouts. I found little, but by the time I disembarked I was fit (thanks to my habit of taking plenty of exercise every day on board) and rested and ready for the discomforts which must surely lie ahead of me.

The discomfort I had expected, but what I had not anticipated was the extraordinary beauty and variety of even this relatively insignificant part of China. It struck me as I went up on deck to supervise the unloading of my trunks and I believe I must have gasped.

A huge pale blue sky hung over a city which was predominantly white and red and gold—a collection of ancient Chinese pagodas and archways mixed with more recent European building. Even these later buildings had a certain magic to them in that light, for they had been built of local stone and much of the stone contained fragments of quartz which glittered when the sun struck them. The European buildings were prominent on the waterfront where many trading companies had built their offices and warehouses and the flags of a score of different Western nations fluttered on masts extended into the streets, while the names of the various companies were emblazoned in their native alphabets and often translated into the beautiful Chinese characters, in black, silver or scarlet.

Chinese officials in flowing robes moved with considerable difficulty through throngs of sweating, near-naked coolies, British and Chinese policemen, soldiers and white-suited Europeans, sailors from a dozen different countries—all mingled casually and with few outward signs of discomfort in what seemed to me, the newcomer, like some huge, dream-like rugger scrum.

A young Chinese boy in a pigtail took me in charge as I left the ship and shepherded me through the throng, finding me a rickshaw and piling me and my luggage aboard until the wickerwork groaned. I put what I hoped was an adequate tip into his outstretched hand and he seemed delighted, for he grinned and bowed many times, uttering the words "God bless, God bless" over and over again before he told the celestial between the rickshaw's shafts that I wanted to go to the Hotel Grasmere, recommended by P. & O. as about the best British hotel in Weihaiwei.

With a lurch the rickshaw set off, and it was with some astonishment that I realized a moment or two later that I was being pulled by a slip of a girl who could not have been much older than sixteen. She made good speed through the crowded, narrow streets of the city and had deposited me outside the Grasmere within twenty minutes.

Again my donation was received with near ecstasy, and it occurred to me that I was probably being over-generous, that a little money would go a very long way for the average Chinese living in Shantung!

The hotel was better than I had expected, with excellent service and pretty modern facilities. The rooms were pleasant and comfortable overlooking an exotic Chinese garden full of small, delicate sculptures, huge, richly coloured blooms and foliage of a score of different shades of green so that the whole thing looked like a jungle fancifully painted by some symbolist aesthete. The scents of the flowers, particularly during the morning and the evening, were overpowering. Electric fans (drawing their energy from the hotel's own up-to-date generator) cooled the rooms, and there were screens at the windows to keep the largest of the insects at bay. I rather regretted I would only be staying a short time in the hotel.

* * *

The morning after my arrival, I paid a visit on the British Consul, a youngish chap connected, I gathered, to one of our best families. A little on the languid, foppish side, he gave the impression of being infinitely bored with China and all things Chinese, but his advice seemed sound and he put me in touch with a local man who made regular trading visits into the hinterland of the province and who agreed, for a sum of money, to escort me all the way to the Valley of the Morning.

This chap was a tall, slightly stooped Chinese of early middle age, who carried himself with the utmost dignity and, while wearing plain cotton garments of the simplest sort, managed to convey the feeling (in me, at least) that he had not always been a mere merchant. I could not help but be reminded of the aristocratic merchant-adventurers of earlier European times and, indeed, it was soon revealed to me that Mr. Lu Kan-fon betrayed a singularly fine command of English and French, knew German and Spanish pretty well and could communicate adequately in Dutch. I also gathered that he had a good knowledge of Japanese. Moreover, he had read a great deal in all of these languages, and, English aside, had a far better familiarity with the literature of those countries than had I. He had been educated, he said, by a European missionary who had taught him much of what he now knew, but I found the explanation inadequate, though I was too polite, of course, to tax him on it. I suspected him of being either a dishonoured aristocrat (perhaps from Peking) or the younger son of an impoverished family. The court intrigues of the Manchus and their followers were notorious and it was quite probable that he had, at some time, played a game of politics in Peking which he had lost. However, it was none of my business if he wished to disguise his past or his origins, and I was relieved for my part to know that I would be traveling in the company of a cultured companion whose English was almost as fluent as my own (I had privately dreaded the difficulties of communicating with a guide in the wilds of China, for my knowledge of Mandarin and Cantonese has never been particularly good).

Mr. Lu told me that his little caravan would not be leaving Weihaiwei for several days, so, accordingly, I spent the rest of the week in the city and did not waste it (as I saw it!) but assiduously enquired of anyone named Bastable, or answering Bastable's description, who might have been there. I received no information of any obvious value, but at least felt content that I had not made the ironic mistake of going off to look for a man who could, by the laws of coincidence, be found living in the next room to mine in the hotel!

At the end of the week I took a rickshaw to Mr. Lu's large and rambling emporium near the centre of the Old Town, bringing with me the bare necessities I would need on the long journey. The rest of the party had already assembled by the time I arrived. They awaited me in a spacious stableyard which reminded me somewhat of a medieval English inn yard. Riding horses and pack animals were being loaded and harnessed, their hoofs churning the ground to mud. Chinese, dressed in stout traveling-garments of heavy cotton, wool and leather, shouted to one another as they worked, and I noted that there was not a man, save for Lu Kan-fon himself, who did not have a serviceable modern rifle over his shoulders and at least one bandolier of cartridges strapped about him.

Lu saw me and came over to instruct his servants in the distribution of my luggage on the pack horses, apologizing for the confusion and the condition of the horse I was to ride (it was a perfectly good beast). I indicated the arms which his men bore.

"I see that you are expecting trouble, Mr. Lu."

He shrugged slightly. "One has to expect trouble in these times, Mr. Moorcock. Those guns, however, should ensure that we see little of it!"

I was relieved that the horsemen were to ride with us. Outside the city I might well have mistaken them for the very bandits we feared. I reflected that if we were to meet any bandits who looked half as fierce as our own men, I would be more than a little perturbed!

At last we set off, Mr. Lu at the head of the caravan. Through the crowded, bustling streets we rode, moving very slowly, for there seemed to be no established right of way—one took one's chances. I was expecting that we would head for the gates of the Old City, but instead we turned towards the more modern sections of the city and eventually arrived at the railway station (which might have been transported stone by stone from London, save for the Chinese words decorating it) and I found that we were riding directly through an archway and on to one of the main platforms where a train was waiting.

Mr. Lu plainly enjoyed my surprise, for he smiled quietly and said: "This first lap will be by train—but in case the train should meet obstacles, we take our horses with us. You call it insurance?"

I smiled back. "I suppose we do."

Horses and riders went directly into waiting goods trucks. I learned from Mr. Lu that our entourage would travel with their animals, while we walked a little further along the train to where a first-class compartment had been prepared for us (Mr. Lu seemed to have considerable influence with the railway company and I gathered that he traveled this route fairly frequently).

We settled into a carriage which would have put most British carriages to shame and were immediately served with tea and light refreshments.

It was then that Mr. Lu, taking mild and humorous pleasure in mystifying me slightly, revealed the destination of the train.

"With luck, we should get as far as Nanking," he told me. "Under ordinary circumstances the journey would not take us more than three days, but we must be prepared for some delays."

"What would be the cause of such delays?" I sipped the delicious tea.

"Oh, there are many causes." He shrugged. "Bandits blow up the lines. Peasants use the sleepers and the sections of rail for their own purposes. Then again there is the general incompetence of the company employees—and that's probably the greatest problem of them all!"

This incompetence was demonstrated very quickly. Our train was due to leave at noon, but in fact did not leave the station until just after four. However, any impatience I might have felt was soon dissipated by the sights of the interior which greeted me after the city was behind us. Immense stretches of flat paddy-fields, interrupted by the occasional low hill around which a village was invariably built, shimmered in the soft light of the Chinese sun. Here was revealed the real, immutable wealth of China— her rice. The value of silver might fluctuate; industries would fail or prosper at the whim of the rest of the world; cities and states could rise and fall; conquerors would come and go, but China's rice and China's hardy peasantry were eternal. That, at any rate, is how it seemed to me then. I had never seen farming of any kind of such a scale as this. For miles and miles in all directions the fields stretched, predominantly green or yellow, intersected with low earthen dykes and somewhat broader ribbons of silver which were the irrigation canals, and above all this was the wide, hazy blue sky in which hung a few wisps of pale, lonely cloud.

The train chugged on, and while the landscape changed hardly at all it did not become boring. There was always something to see—a little group of scantily dressed peasants in their wide-brimmed straw hats and their pigtails, waving cheerfully to the train (I always waved back!)—a sampan making its way slowly up a canal—an ancient bridge which looked like a perfect work of art to me and yet which was plainly just a bridge built for an ordinary road between one tiny township and another. Sometimes, too, I saw pagodas, small walled cities (some virtually in ruins) with those highly ornate many-tiered gates typical of Chinese architecture, houses decorated with red and green tiles, with ceramic statuary, with bronzework and with mirror glass which made some of them seem as if they burned with a strange silver fire. When the train came, as it frequently did, to a sudden jerking stop, I had plenty of opportunities to study these sights in detail. It was on the third day, when we had made something over half of our journey to Nanking, that I began to notice significant changes in the demeanour of the people in the towns and villages we passed. The peasants rarely waved to the trains and were inclined to look upon us with a certain amount of apprehension and even downright suspicion. Moreover, it soon became obvious that there were a great many people about who were not local to the areas. I saw several detachments of cavalry on the roads we passed, and once thought I saw an infantry division moving through the paddy-fields. Elsewhere there was evidence of, at very least, some sort of martial law in operation—more than once I saw peasants being stopped, questioned and searched by men in uniforms of a variety of descriptions. There was no question in my mind that this part of China was being disputed over, probably by at least three factions, amongst them the central authority. I had heard tales of the petty warlords who had sprung up in the last few years, claiming all sorts of honours, titles and rights— each one claimed to represent the forces of law and order, none would admit to being little more than a rapacious bandit—now it looked as if I was witnessing the truth of the tales for myself. The long journey to Nanking passed without incident, however, and we disembarked from the train with some relief.

Nanking is a great and splendid city (if a little dilapidated here and there) and deserves a fuller description than I have space for. It is the capital of Kiangsu Province and one of China's major cities (it has, on occasions, been the capital). It lies at the foot of an impressive range of mountains whose slopes are thickly wooded and richly cultivated with terraced fields, and it is built on the banks of the mighty Yangtze Kiang river. It is at once one of China's most ancient cities and one of the most modern—ideal for trade, surrounded by some of the most fertile agricultural land in the world, it has a number of flourishing industries. Its financiers are famous for their wealth and their power and Nanking cuisine is highly regarded. In contrast to most Chinese towns, Nanking's ramparts are irregular, spreading from the river, along the banks of Lake Xuan-wu, to the Hill of the Rain of Flowers. The naval shipyards and the market places are on the west of the city, between the ramparts and the river. Again one finds a strange mixture of the old Chinese architecture—impressive, complicated buildings embellished with intricate ceramic work—and more modern buildings, some of them very dull, but some of them wonders of late Victorian Gothic which, fortunately, is beginning to disappear in Europe to be replaced by the more gracious architecture of those influenced by the Art Nouveau movements. There is much shipping on the river—sampans, junks and steamers used for every possible purpose—as ferry-boats, trading vessels, military craft and so on. There is a racecourse, an immense number of gardens, some large and ornate, some small and simple. There are libraries, museums, schools and art galleries, the consulates of all the great European Powers, luxurious hotels, temples, palaces, wide avenues lined with trees. I regretted greatly that our stay there was not to be longer, and made the best use of my time while Lu conducted his business, seeing as much of interest in the city as possible. I also called the British Consulate to apprehend them of my movements, enquire after Bastable and collect some cash I had arranged to be cabled there.

The second stage of our journey was by steamer, and still the horses had not been used! I began to envy the beasts—they seemed to be the most underworked animals I had ever come across. Stables had been prepared for them in the hold of the big paddle-steamer and they seemed content to return to their cramped quarters while Lu and myself retired to the merchant's stateroom where lunch was immediately forthcoming. The steamer left on time and we were soon heading up the broad Yangtze Kiang on our way to Wuchang, which would be our next stopping-place. I was fretting somewhat, for the journey was extremely roundabout, yet I was assured by Mr. Lu that this was the safest route and the one most likely to get me to my ultimate destination, for this part of China in particular was in a highly unstable political state. He had learned, in fact, that an army under General Zhang Xun was rumoured to be advancing on the city and that there might well be heavy fighting in the outskirts. I had noted the number of soldiers occupying the streets around the centre and could well believe that we had narrowly missed being mixed up in a war.

At any other time I would have been delighted to have remained there and witnessed the sport, but it was important to me that Bastable be located and I could not risk losing as competent a guide and traveling companion as Lu Kan-fon. I had heard something of General Zhang Xun and gathered that he was a rascal of the first water, that his men had created terrible havoc in other parts of the province, stealing anything they could lay hands on, burning villages, molesting women and so forth.

Soon Nanking and her problems had disappeared behind us and it seemed that we were the only moving object in the whole wide world at times, for as the river broadened we saw fewer and fewer other vessels. The paddles of the steamer swept us along slowly but surely with a heartening and steady beat. Our smoke drifted low behind us, hanging over the water which was sometimes deep and blue, sometimes shallow and yellow. There were hills on both sides of us now and the variety of shades of green would have put even the lovely English landscape to shame. Indeed I was reminded of the English landscape the more I saw of China. The only difference was the scale. What would have been a view stretching for a mile or two in England became a scene stretching for scores of miles in China! Like England, too, there was a sense of most of the landscape having been nurtured and cultivated for all of Time, used but used lovingly and with respect for its natural appearance.

It was on the third day of our journey upriver that the first serious incident took place. I was leaning on the rail of the ship, looking towards the west bank (which was closest) and enjoying my first pipe of the day when I suddenly heard a sharp report and, looking in the direction from which the sound had seemed to come, noticed a white puff of smoke. Peering more carefully, I made out several riders armed with rifles. More reports followed and I heard something whizz through the rigging over my head. I realized that we were being shot at and hastily ran along the deck to the wheelhouse with the intention of warning the Dutch skipper of the boat.

Old Cornelius, the skipper, smiled at me as I told him what was happening.

"Best stay inside, den, *Minheer*," he said, puffing phlegmatically on his own pipe, his huge red face running with sweat, for it was all but airless in the wheelhouse.

"Should we not pull further out into midstream?" I enquired. "We are surely in some danger."

"Oh, yes, in danger ve are, most certainly, but ve should be in much greater danger if ve vent further to midstream. De currents—dey are very strong, sir. Ve must just hope dat not'in' serious is hit, eh? Dey are alvays shootin' at us, dese days. Any powered vessel is suspected off bein' a military ship."

"Who are they? Can we not report them to the nearest authorities?"

"Dey could easily *be* de aut'orities, *Minheer*." Cornelius laughed and patted me on the shoulder. "Do not vorry, eh?"

I took his advice. After all, there was little else I could do! And soon the danger was past.

Nothing of a similar nature happened to us in the course of the next couple of days. Once I saw a whole town on fire. Lurid red flames lit up the dusk and thick, heavy smoke drifted over the river to mingle with ours. I saw panic-stricken people trying to crowd into sampans, while others hailed us from the bank, trying to get us to help them, but the skipper would have none of it, claiming that it was suicide to stop and that we should be overrun. I saw his logic, but I felt a dreadful pang, for we sailed close enough to be able to see, with the aid of field-glasses, the fear-racked faces of the women and children. Many women stood up to their waists in water, holding their infants to them and screaming at us to help. The following morning I saw several detachments of cavalry in the uniforms of the central government, riding hell-for-leather along the bank, while behind them rode either irregulars attached to them, or pursuers, it was hard to tell. In the afternoon I saw field artillery being drawn by six-horse teams over a tall bridge spanning a particularly narrow section of the Yangtze Kiang. It had obviously been involved in a fierce engagement, for the soldiers were weary, wounded and scorched, while the wheels and barrels of the guns were thick with mud and there were signs that the guns had been fired almost to destruction (I saw only one ammunition tender and guessed that the others, empty, had been abandoned). Framed against the redness of the setting sun, the detachment looked as if it had returned from Hell itself.

I was glad to reach Wuchang, but somewhat nervous concerning the next stage of our journey, which would be overland by horse, backtracking to an extent, along the river and then in the general direction of Shancheng—unless we could get a train as far as Kwang Shui. It was what we had originally hoped to do, but we had heard rumours that the line to Kwang Shui had been blown up by bandits.

Wuchang faces the point where the Han Ho river merges with the Yangtze Kiang. It is one of three large towns lying close to each other, and of them Wuchang is the loveliest. Hanyang and Hankow are beginning to take on a distinctly European character, giving themselves over increasingly to industry and ship-building. But there was no real rest in Wuchang. Martial law had been declared and a mood of intense gloom hung over the whole city. Moreover, it had begun to rain—a thin drizzle which somehow managed to soak through almost any clothing one wore and chilled one to the very bone. The various officials who appeared at the dock as we came in were over-zealous in checking our papers and sorting through our baggage, suspecting us, doubtless, of being revolutionists or bandits. The better hotels had been taken over almost entirely by high-ranking officers and we were forced at last to put up at a none-too-clean inn near the quays, and even here there were a good many soldiers to keep us awake with their drunken carousing into the night. I pitied any town they might be called upon to defend!

Mr. Lu disappeared very early the next morning and returned while I was eating an unpalatable breakfast of rice and some kind of stew which had been served to me with genuine apologies on the part of our host. There was little else, he said. The soldiers had eaten everything—and no-one was paying him.

Mr. Lu looked pleased with himself and soon took the opportunity to let me know that he had managed to secure passage for us on the next train leaving Wuchang. The train was chiefly a troop transport, but would take a certain number of boxcars. If I did not mind the discomfort of traveling with the men and horses, we could leave almost immediately.

I was glad to agree and we gathered up our luggage and went to meet the rest of our party on the far side of town where they had been camped, sleeping in the open, curled up against their steeds. They looked red-eyed and angry and were cursing at each other as they saddled up and prepared the baggage for the pack animals.

We made our way to the station in something of a hurry, for there was precious little time. Mr. Lu said that a troop transport was more likely to leave on time—or even ahead of time if it was ready to go. The army could decide.

We got to the station and the train was still in—drawn by one of the largest locomotives I have ever seen. It belonged to no class I recognized, was painted a mixture of bright blue and orange, and was bellowing more fire and smoke than Siegfried's dragon.

We crowded into the boxcars, the doors were shut on us, and off we jerked, hanging on for dear life as the train gathered speed.

Later we were able to get one of the sliding doors partly open and look out. We were in high mountain country, winding our way steadily upwards through some of the loveliest country I have ever seen in my life. Old, old mountains, clothed in verdant trees, the very image of those Chinese paintings which seem so formalized until you have seen the original of what the artist described. And then you realize that it is Nature herself who is formalized in China, that the country has been populated so long that there is scarcely a blade of grass, growing in no matter what remote spot, which has not in some way received the influence of Man. And here, as in other parts of China, the wilderness is not made any less impressive by this imprint. If anything, it is made more impressive. Mr. Lu shared my pleasure in the sight (though he took a somewhat condescending, proprietorial attitude towards me as I gasped and exclaimed and wondered).

"I expected to be delighted with China," I told him. "But I am more than delighted. I am overawed—and my faith in the beauties of Nature is restored forever!"

Mr. Lu said nothing, but a little later he took out his cigarette case and, offering me a fine Turkish, remarked that even Nature at her most apparently invulnerable was still in danger from the works of mankind.

I had been thinking of Bastable and his description of the

bomb which had blown him back into his own time, and I must admit that I gave Mr. Lu a hard look, wondering if perhaps he knew more of Bastable than he had said, but he added nothing to this remark and I decided to accept it for one of generalized philosophy.

Accepting the cigarette, I nodded. "That's true. I sincerely hope this civil strife does not destroy too much of your country," I said, leaning forward to give him a match. The train swayed as it took a bend and revealed to me a lush forest, full of the subtlest greens I had ever seen. "For I have fallen in love with China."

"Unfortunately," said Mr. Lu in a dry but good-humoured tone, "you are not the only European to be so smitten. But must one always take steps to *possess* that which one loves, Mr. Moorcock?"

I accepted his point. "I do not approve of my government's Chinese policies," I told him. "But you will admit that there is more law and order in the territories controlled by Britain than in other parts of China. After all, the Chinese Question remains a vexed one…"

"There would be no Chinese Question, Mr. Moorcock," said Mr. Lu with a ghost of a smile, "without Europe and Japan. Who was it introduced massive importation of opium into our country? Who was responsible for the devaluation of our currency? These were not internally created problems."

"Probably not. And yet…"

"And yet I could be wrong. Who is to tell?"

"The Manchus cannot be said to be incorruptible," I told him, and I smiled a smile which echoed his.

His own smile became a broad grin and he sat back against the wall, waving the hand which held the cigarette, granting me, as it were, the match. I think the gesture was made graciously rather than from any real agreement with the point of view I had presented.

* * *

The train traveled steadily through the rest of the day and into the night. We slept as best we could on the shuddering floor of the wagon, ever in danger of a horse breaking free and trampling us. It was almost dawn when the train came to a sudden screaming halt, causing the horses to buck about in fear, stamping and snorting, causing our men to leap to their feet, hands on their rifles.

The noise of the stop gave way to a peculiar and uncanny silence. In the distance we heard a few voices shouting back along the train and cautiously we slid the doors right back, peering into the murk to try to see what was happening.

"At least there's no gunfire," said Mr. Lu calmly. "We are not under direct attack. Perhaps it is nothing more than a blockage on the line."

But it was plain he was not convinced by his own suggestion. Together we clambered from the wagon and began to walk up the line towards the locomotive.

The big engine was still ejaculating huge clouds of white steam and through this steam moved dark figures. From the windows of the carriages there poked scores of heads as sleepy soldiers shouted enquiries or exchanged speculations about the reasons for our stopping.

Mr. Lu singled out one of the more competent-looking officers and addressed a few short questions to him. The man replied, shrugging frequently, making dismissive gestures, pointing towards the north and up at the jagged mountain peaks above our heads.

The sun made its first tentative appearance as Mr. Lu rejoined me.

"The line has been blown up," he said. "We are lucky that the driver acted with alacrity in stopping the train. There is no chance of continuing. The train will have to go back to the nearest town. We have the choice of going with it and enjoying the dubious security of traveling with these soldiers, or we can continue our journey on horseback."

I made up my mind immediately, for I was slowly becoming impatient with the delays and diversions we had so far experienced. "I should like to continue," I told Mr. Lu. "It is time those horses were exercised!"

This was evidently the answer he had hoped for. With a quick smile he turned and began to stride back to our section of the train, calling out to his men to ready the horses and to load them, saying to me in an English aside:

"Personally I think we stand a much better chance on our own. This is territory at present controlled by the warlord General Liu Fang. His main interest is in wiping out the troops which have been sent against him. I do not think he will bother an ordinary caravan, particularly if we have a European gentleman traveling with us. Liu Fang hopes, I gather, to recruit allies from Europe. A plan which is almost certainly doomed to failure, but it will be of help to us."

Accordingly, we were soon on horseback, heading down the long slope away from the stranded train. By noon we were deep into unpopulated country, following the course of a river along the floor of a valley. The valley was narrow and thickly wooded and at length we were forced to dismount and lead our horses through the moss-covered rocks. It had begun to rain quite heavily and the ground was slippery, slowing our progress even more. Moreover, it had become hard to see more than a few yards ahead of us. Owing to my lack of sleep and the hypnotic effect of the rain falling on the foliage above my head, I continued almost in a trance, hardly aware of my own tiredness. We exchanged few words and emerged from the forest and remounted when it was quite late in the afternoon, with only a few hours of daylight left. The river began to rise and we still followed it, from one valley into another, until we came upon some reasonably level ground where we decided to make camp and consult our maps to see what progress we had so far made.

It was as I watched the men erecting the tent which Lu and I would share that I glanced up into the hills and thought I saw a figure move behind a rock some distance away. I remarked on this to Mr. Lu. He accepted that I had probably seen someone, but he reassured me.

"It is not surprising. Probably only an observer—a scout sent to keep an eye on us and make sure that we are not a disguised military expedition. I doubt if we shall be bothered by him."

I could not sleep well that night and I must admit that in my exhaustion I had begun to regret the impulse which had sent me on this adventure. I wondered if it would all end in some sordid massacre, if, by morning, my stripped corpse would lie amongst the remains of our camp. I would not be the first European foolish enough to embark upon such a journey and pay the ultimate price for his folly. When I did sleep, at last, my dreams were not pleasant. Indeed, they were the strangest and most terrifying dreams I have ever experienced. Yet, for some reason, I awoke from all this feeling completely refreshed and cleansed of my fears. I began to be optimistic about our chances of reaching the Valley of the Morning and ate the crude fare served us for breakfast with immense relish.

Mr. Lu was moved to comment on my demeanour. "We Chinese are famous for our stoicism," he said, "but we could learn something from your British variety!"

"It's not stoicism," I said. "Merely a mood. I can't explain it."

"Perhaps you sense good luck. I hope so." He indicated the rocky hills on both sides of us. "A fairly large company of men has been moved up in the night. We are probably completely surrounded."

"Do they mean to attack, I wonder?" I glanced about, but could see no sign of the soldiers.

"I would suppose that this manoeuvre is a precaution. They are probably still wondering if we are spies or part of a disguised army."

I now noticed that our men were betraying a certain nervousness, fingering their rifles and bandoliers, glancing around them at the rocks and muttering amongst themselves in an agitated fashion. Lu Kan-fon was the only person who seemed unconcerned; speaking rapidly, he gave orders for our pack horses to be loaded and, at first reluctantly, his men moved to obey. It was only when the last bundle had been secured and we prepared to mount that the soldiers revealed themselves.

Unlike many of the government troops, these men wore uniforms which were distinctly Chinese—loose smocks and trousers of black, yellow, white and red. On the backs and fronts of the smocks were big circles on which had been printed Chinese characters, evidently giving the rank and regiment of the soldier. Some wore skull-caps, while others had wide-brimmed straw hats. All were clean-shaven and well-disciplined and all possessed modern carbines, apparently of German manufacture. While their guns were pointed at us, they were held at the hip rather than at the shoulder, denoting that no immediate harm was intended to us. Immediately, Mr. Lu held up his hand and ordered his men not to touch their own weapons, whereupon there emerged from behind a large bush a mounted figure of such splendid appearance that I thought at first he must surely be arrayed for a festival.

He rode his shaggy pony slowly down the hillside towards us. He must have been well over six feet in height and with massive shoulders and chest. He was wearing a long brocade gown embroidered for about a foot round the bottom with waves of the sea and other Chinese devices. Over this was a long satin coat with an embroidered breastplate and a similar square of embroidery on the back, with the horseshoe cuffs, forced upon the Chinese by the Manchus when the present dynasty came to the throne, falling over his hands. High official boots, an amber necklace of very large beads reaching to his waist and aureole-shaped official cap with large red tassel, completed the costume. There was a large sword at his side, but no other visible arms, and he guided his pony with one hand while keeping the other on the hilt of the sword, somehow managing to retain an impressive dignity while the horse picked its way down to where we waited, virtually frozen in position.

His face was expressionless as he rode into our camp and brought his mount to a halt, looking us over through his slanting, jet-black eyes. Mr. Lu and myself came in for a particularly close examination, and it was while the man was inspecting me that I decided to try to break the atmosphere and bowed slightly, saying in English:

"Good morning, sir. I am a British citizen on a private journey with these traders. I regret it if we have inadvertently entered territory which you would prefer to remain untraveled…"

My rather mealy-mouthed speech was interrupted by a grunt from the magnificent rider, who ignored me and addressed Mr. Lu in flowing Mandarin.

"You know who I am? You know where you are? What is your excuse for being here?"

Mr. Lu bowed low before speaking. "I know who you are, honourable one, and I most humbly ask your forgiveness for giving you the trouble of needing to inspect our little caravan. But we were traveling by train until yesterday when the train met an obstacle and was forced to return to the nearest town. We decided to continue overland…"

"You were seen leaving the troop train. You are spies, are you not?"

"Not at all, mighty General Liu Fang. The troop train was the only available transport. We are merchants: we are on our way to trade in Shantung."

"Who is the foreigner?"

"An Englishman. A writer who wishes to write a book about our country."

At this quick-witted piece of invention the legendary General Liu Fang showed a flicker of interest. He also appeared slightly mollified, for he had no reason to suspect I was anything but a neutral party in his territory (as, of course, I was) and probably thought it might be in his interest to cultivate the goodwill of one of the foreigners whose aid he was rumoured to be seeking.

"Tell your men to disarm themselves," he ordered, and Mr. Lu relayed the order at once. Scowling, his men unslung their guns and dropped them to the ground.

"And where is your immediate destination?" said the general to me in halting French.

I replied in the same tongue. "I have heard of a particularly beautiful valley in these parts. It is called the Valley of the Morning." I saw no point in beating about the bush, particularly since I might not have another opportunity to discover the exact whereabouts of my destination for some time.

General Liu Fang plainly recognized the name, but his reaction was strange. He frowned heavily and darted a deeply suspicious look at me. "Who do you seek there?"

"No one in particular," said I. "My interest in the place is purely, as it were, geographical." I, in turn, noting his reaction, had become cautious of revealing anything more.

He seemed to relax, momentarily satisfied with my reply. "I would advise you against visiting the valley," he said. "There are bandits in the area."

I wondered to myself sardonically what he called himself, but of course let nothing of this show on my face as I said: "I am grateful for the warning. Perhaps with the protection of your army…"

He gestured impatiently. "I am fighting a war, *monsieur*. I cannot spare men to escort foreign journalists about the country."

"I apologize," I said, and bowed again.

There was still considerable tension in the situation and I noted that the soldiers had not relaxed but were still pointing their rifles at us. There must have been at least a hundred of them in well-protected positions on both sides of the valley. The general returned his attention to Mr. Lu. "What goods do you carry for trade?"

Mr. Lu had folded his arms. He said impassively: "Many kinds. Mainly articles of artistic interest. Statuettes, ceramics and the like."

"They will be inspected," said the general. "Instruct your men to unload the goods."

Again Mr. Lu obeyed without demur. As his men began to unpack the bundles which they had so recently strapped onto the pack horses, he said to me in English: "We might escape with our lives, but not, I fear, our possessions…"

"Silence!" said the general firmly. He rode forward to where Mr. Lu's goods had been laid out, looked them over with the shrewd eye of a Chinese peasant woman inspecting fish in a market and then rode back to where we stood. "They will be requisitioned," he said, "to help us win freedom from the Manchus."

Fatalistically, Mr. Lu bowed. "A worthy cause," he said dryly. "The horses—?"

"The horses will also be requisitioned. They will be of particular use…"

It was at this point that he was interrupted by the sound of machine-gun fire and I thought at first that he had somehow given the signal for our slaughter. But the gunfire came from higher up the hillside and I saw at once that it was his men who were the target for the attack. My spirits lifted. Surely these must be government troops coming to our rescue!

My relief was shortlived. Almost at once General Liu Fang shouted an order to his men and, head well down over the neck of his horse, spurred rapidly for the cover of some nearby rocks.

It had begun to rain suddenly—a heavy, misty rain which

acted like fog to obscure visibility—and I had no idea of what was happening, save that the general's troops were firing on us.

Mr. Lu's men dived for their own weapons, but half of them were cut down before they could reach their rifles. Those who remained snatched up their guns and sought what cover they could. Mr. Lu grabbed my arm and together we ran towards a depression in the ground where we might escape the worst of the concentrated fire from above. We flung ourselves down and buried our faces in the soft moss while the three-sided battle went on all around us. I remember noting that the machine-guns kept up an incredibly efficient chattering and I wondered how any Chinese army could have acquired such artillery (for the Chinese are notorious for the poor quality of their arms and their inefficiency in maintaining those that they have).

Bullets thudded about us and I expected to be hit at any moment. I shouted over the noise of gunfire and the cries of the wounded. "Who are they, Mr. Lu?"

"I do not know, Mr. Moorcock. All I do know is that whereas we might have escaped with our lives, we now stand a very good chance of being killed. They doubtless consider it more important to destroy General Liu Fang than to save us!" He laughed. "I regret that I shall be forced to return your fee—I have not kept my part of the bargain. Your chances of finding the Valley of the Morning have become exceptionally slender. My protection has proved inadequate!"

"I am forced to agree with you, Mr. Lu," said I, and would have continued had I not recognized the distinctive sound of a bullet striking flesh and bone. I lifted my head, thinking at first that I had been hit, but it was Mr. Lu. He must have died instantly, for he had been shot not once but twice, almost simultaneously, in the head.

I had an immediate sense of grief, realizing how much I had enjoyed the sophisticated company of the Chinese, but the sight of his ruined head sickened me and I was forced to avert my eyes.

The death of Mr. Lu seemed to be a signal for the fighting to stop. Shortly afterwards the sound of gunfire ended and I lifted my head cautiously to peer through the drifting rain. Death was everywhere. Our own men lay amongst the scattered and broken remains of the works of art they had carried for so long and so far. A few had once again laid down their weapons and were raising their hands high above their heads. General Liu Fang was nowhere to be seen (I learned later he had kept riding, abandoning his men to their fate), but the warlord's soldiers lay in postures of death everywhere I looked. I rose, raising my own hands. There came a few more isolated shots and I surmised that, in Chinese fashion, the wounded were being finished off.

I must have waited for at least ten minutes before I got my first sight of our 'rescuers'. They were all mounted, all wearing leather caps of a distinctively Mongolian appearance and all carried light rifles of a decidedly unfamiliar pattern. Their loose shirts were of silk or cotton and some wore leather capes to protect themselves against the worst of the rain, while others wore quilted jackets. They were mainly good-looking Northern Chinese, tall and somewhat arrogant in their bearing, and none had pigtails. Most had armbands as their only insignia—a fanciful design consisting of a circle from which radiated eight slender arrows. I knew at once that they could not, after all, be government troops, but were doubtless some rival bandit army either fighting for themselves or allied with the government troops against General Liu Fang.

And then their leader rode into sight from out of the misty rain. I knew it must be the leader from the way in which the other riders fell back. Also it was rare to see a handsome black Arab stallion in these parts and that was what the leader rode. Slender, a graceful rider, dressed in a long black leather topcoat with a narrow waist and a flaring skirt, a broad-brimmed leather hat hiding the face, a long Cossack-style sabre hanging from a belt of elaborately ornamented silk, the bandit chief rode towards me, lifted the brim of the hat away from the face and showed evident, and almost childish, amusement at my astonishment.

"Good morning, Mr. Moorcock."

Her voice was clear and well-modulated—the voice of an educated Englishwoman (though bearing perhaps the slightest trace of an accent). She was young, no older than thirty at very most, and she had a pale, soft complexion. Her eyes were grey-blue and her mouth was wide and full-lipped. She had an oval face which would have been merely pretty had it not been for the character in it. As it was, I thought her the most beautiful woman I had ever seen. Her slightly waving black hair was short, framing her face but barely touching her shoulders.

And all I could blurt out was: "How do you know my name?"

She laughed. "Our intelligence is rather better than General Liu Fang's. I am sorry so many of your men were killed—and I particularly regret the death of Mr. Lu. Though he did not know that it was I who attacked, we were old friends and I had been looking forward to meeting him again."

"You take his death rather casually," I said.

"It was a casual death. I have not introduced myself. My name is Una Persson. For some months we have been harassed by General Liu and this is the first opportunity we have had to teach him a lesson. We were originally coming to find you and take you with us to the Valley of the Morning, but I could not afford to miss the chance of ambushing such a large number of the general's troops."

"How did you know I sought the Valley of the Morning?"

"I have known for at least a month. You have made many enquiries."

"Your name is familiar—where have I heard it…?" Slowly it dawned on me. "Bastable mentioned you! The woman on the airship—the revolutionist. Una Persson!"

"I am an acquaintance of Captain Bastable."

My heart leapt. "Is he there? Is he in the Valley of the Morning as I suspected?"

"He has been there," she agreed. "And he has left something of himself behind."

"But Bastable? What of him? I am anxious to speak to him. Where is he now?"

And then this mysterious woman made the most cryptic utterance she had made so far. She shrugged and gave a little, tired smile, pulling on her horse's reins so that the beast began to move away. "Where indeed?" she said. "It is not a question easily answered, Mr. Moorcock, for we are all nomads of the time streams…"

I stood there, puzzled, chilled, miserable and too weary to question her further. She rode to where Mr. Lu's goods lay scattered about and beneath the corpses of men and horses. She dismounted and stooped to inspect one shattered figurine, dipped her finger into the hollow which had been revealed and lifted the finger to her nose. She nodded to herself as if confirming something she had already known. Then she began to give orders to her men in rapid Cantonese dialect which I could scarcely follow at all. Carefully, they gathered up both the fragments and the few figurines which were still unbroken. It did not take a particularly subtle intelligence to put two and two together. Now I knew why Mr. Lu had taken such an oddly circuitous route and why he had been eager to leave the troop train as soon as possible. Plainly, he was an opium smuggler. I found it hard to believe that such an apparently decent and well-educated man could indulge in so foul a trade, but the evidence was indisputable. For some reason I could not find it in my heart to loathe the dead man and I guessed that some sort of perverted idealism had led him to this means of making money. I also had an explanation of the general's interest in Mr. Lu's goods—doubtless the bandit chief had guessed the truth, which was why he had been so eager to "requisition" the articles.

The booty was collected quickly and Una Persson mounted her sleek stallion without another glance at me, riding off through the rain. One of her silent warriors brought me a horse and signaled for me to climb into the saddle. I did so with eagerness, for I had no intention of becoming separated from the beautiful bandit leader—she was my first real link with Bastable and there was every chance she would take me to him. I felt no danger from these rascals and had an inkling that Una Persson was, if not sympathetic, at least neutral with regard to me.

Thus, surrounded by her men, I followed behind her as we left that little vale of death and the remnants of Mr. Lu's party and cantered along a narrow track which wound higher and higher into the mountains.

I was hardly aware of the details of that journey, so eaten up was I with curiosity. A thousand questions seethed in my skull— how could a woman who had been described by Bastable as being young in the year 1973 be here, apparently just as young, in the year 1910? Once again I experienced that almost fearful *frisson* which I had experienced when listening to Bastable's speculations on the paradoxes of Time.

And would Democratic Dawn City—Chi'ng Che'eng Ta-Chia—that secret Utopian revolutionary citadel be there when we arrived in the Valley of the Morning?

And why was Una Persson taking part in China's internecine politics? Why did these tall, silent men follow her?

I hoped that I would have at least some answers to these questions when we arrived in the Valley of the Morning, but, as it emerged, I was to be in several ways disappointed.

It was after dark by the time that we reached Una Persson's camp and the rain had fallen ceaselessly, so that it was still difficult to make out details, but it was obvious that this was no City of the

Future—merely the ruins of a small Chinese township with a few houses still inhabitable. For the most part, however, the soldiers and their women and children lived in makeshift shelters erected in the ruins, while others had set up tents or temporary huts similar to the Mongolian yurt. Cooking-fires guttered here and there amongst the fallen masonry and half-burned timbers which spoke of some disaster having befallen the town fairly recently. Much of the ground had been churned to mud and was made even more treacherous by the arrival of our horses. As I dismounted, Una Persson rode up and pointed with a riding-crop at one of the still-standing houses.

"You'll be my guest for supper, I hope, Mr. Moorcock."

"You are kind, madam," I replied. "But I fear I am not properly dressed to take supper with such a beautiful hostess…"

She grinned at the compliment. "You are picking up Chinese habits of speech, I see. Your clothes were rescued. You'll find them in your room. San Chui here will show you where it is. You'll be able to wash there, too. Until later, then." She saluted me with the crop and rode off to supervise the unloading of her spoils (which also consisted of most of the weapons which had a short while ago belonged to Mr. Lu's and the general's men). I had an opportunity to see one of the machine-guns I had initially only heard and was astonished that it was so light and yet so capable of dealing out death with extraordinary efficiency. This, too, was of a completely unfamiliar pattern. Indeed, it was the sort of weapon I might have expected to find in a city of the future!

San Chui, impassive as his comrades, bowed and led the way into the house, which was carpeted in luxurious style throughout but was otherwise of a somewhat Spartan appearance. In a room near the top of the house I found my baggage and my spare suit already laid out on my sleeping-mat (there was no bed). Shortly afterwards another soldier, who had changed into a smock and trousers of blue linen, brought me a bowl of hot water and I was able to get the worst of the mud and dust off my person, find a reasonably uncrumpled shirt, don the fresh suit and walk down to supper safe in the conviction that I was able to make at least an approximate appearance of civilized demeanour!

I was to dine alone, it seemed, with my hostess. She herself had changed into a simple gown of midnight-blue silk, trimmed with scarlet in the Chinese fashion. With her short hair and her oval face she looked, in the light of the candles burning on the dining-table, almost Chinese. She wore no ornament and there was no trace of paint on her face, yet she looked even more beautiful than the first time I had seen her. When I bowed it was instinctively, in homage to that beauty. The ground-floor room held the minimum of furniture—a couple of chests against the walls and a low Chinese table at which one sat cross-legged on cushions to eat.

Without enquiry, she handed me a glass of Madeira and I thanked her. Sipping the wine, I found it to be amongst the very best of its kind and I complimented her on it.

She smiled. "Don't praise my taste, Mr. Moorcock. Praise that of the French missionary who ordered it in Shanghai—and who is still, I suppose, wondering what has become of it!"

I was surprised by her easy (even shameless) admission of her banditry, but said nothing. Never having been a great supporter of the established Church, I continued to sip the missionary's wine with relish, however, and found myself relaxing for the first time since I had left civilization. Although I had so many questions to ask her, I discovered myself to be virtually tongue-tied, not knowing where to begin and hoping that she would illuminate me without my having to introduce the subject, say, of Bastable and how she came to know him. The last I had heard of her she had been aboard the airship which had, in the year 1973, dropped a bomb of immense power upon the city of Hiroshima. For the first time I began to doubt

Bastable's story and wonder if, indeed, he had been describing nothing but an opium dream which had become confused with reality to the extent that he had introduced actual people he had known into it.

We seated ourselves to eat and I decided to begin in a somewhat elliptical manner, enquiring, as I sampled the delicious soup (served, in Western fashion, before the main courses): "Any news of your father, Captain Korzeniowski?"

It was her turn to frown in puzzlement, and then her brow cleared and she laughed. "Aha! Of course—Bastable. Oh, Korzeniowski is fine, I think. Bastable spoke well of you—he seemed to trust you. Indeed, the reason that you are here at all is that he asked me to do a favour for him."

"A favour?"

"More of that later. Let us enjoy our meal—this is a luxury for me, you know. Recently we have not had the leisure or the means to prepare elaborate meals."

Once again she had politely—almost sweetly—blocked my questions. I decided to proceed on a new tack.

"This village has sustained a bombardment by the look of it," I said. "Have you been attacked?"

She answered vaguely. "It was attacked, yes. By General Liu, I believe, before we arrived. But one gets used to ruins. This is better than some I have known." Her eyes held a distant, moody look, as if she were remembering other times, other ruins. Then she shrugged and her expression changed. "The world you know is a stable world, Mr. Moorcock, is it not?"

"Comparatively," I said. "Though there are always threats, I suppose. I have sometimes wondered what social stability is. It is probably just a question of points of view and personal experience. My own outlook is a relatively cheerful one. If I were, say, a Jewish immigrant in London's East End, it would probably not be anything like as optimistic!"

She appreciated the remark and smiled. "Well, at least you accept that there *are* other views of society. Perhaps that is why Bastable talked to you; why he liked you."

"Liked me? It is not the impression I received. He disappeared, you know, after our meeting on Rowe Island—without any warning at all. I was concerned for him. He was under a great strain. That, I suppose, is the main reason why I am here. Have you seen him recently? Is he well?"

"I have seen him. He was well enough. But he is trapped—he is probably trapped forever." Her next phrase was addressed to herself, I thought. "Trapped forever in the shifting tides of Time."

I waited for her to elaborate, but she did not. "Bastable will tell you more of that," she said.

"Then he *is* here?"

She shook her head and her hair swayed like the branches of a willow in the wind. She returned her attention to the meal and did not speak for a while as we ate.

Now I had the strange impression that I was not quite real to her, that she spoke to me as she might speak to her horse or a household pet or a familiar picture on her wall, as if she did not expect me to understand and spoke only to clarify her own thoughts. I felt a little uncomfortable, just as someone might feel who was an unwilling eavesdropper on an intimate conversation. Yet I was determined to receive at least some clarification from her.

"I gather that you intend to take me to Bastable—or that Bastable is due to return here?"

"Really? No, no. I am sorry if I have misled you. I have many things on my mind at present. China's problems alone... The historical implications... The possibility of so much going wrong... Whether we should be interfering at all... If we *are* interfering, or only think we are..." She lifted her head and her wonderful eyes stared deep into mine. "Many concerns—

responsibilities—and I am very tired, Mr. Moorcock. It is going to be a long century."

I was completely nonplussed and decided myself to finish the conversation. "Perhaps we can talk in the morning," I said, "when we are both more rested."

"Perhaps," she agreed. "You are going to bed?"

"If you do not think it impolite. The dinner was splendid."

"Yes, it was good. The morning…"

I wondered if she, like Bastable, was also a slave to opium. There was a trance-like quality in her eyes now. She could hardly understand me.

"Until the morning, then," I said.

"Until the morning." She echoed my words almost mindlessly.

"Goodnight, Mrs. Persson."

"Goodnight."

I made my way back upstairs, undressed, lay myself down on the sleeping-mat and, it seemed to me, was immediately dreaming those peculiar, frightening dreams of the previous night. Again, in the morning, I felt completely refreshed and purged. I got up, washed in cold water, dressed and went downstairs. The room was as I had left it—the remains of the previous night's dinner were still on the table. And I was suddenly seized with the conviction that everything had been abandoned hastily—that I had also been abandoned. I walked outside into a fine, pale morning. The rain had stopped and the air smelled fresh and clean. I looked for signs of activity and found nothing. The only life I could see in the village consisted of one horse, saddled and ready to ride. Soldiers, women and children had all disappeared. Now I wondered if, inadvertently, *I* had sampled some of Mr. Lu's opium and had dreamed the whole thing! I went back into the house calling out:

"Mrs. Persson! Mrs. Persson!"

There were only echoes. Not one human being remained in the ruined village.

I went out again. In the distance the low green hills of the Valley of the Morning were soft, gentle and glowing after the rain which must have stopped in the night. A large, watery sun hung in the sky. Birds sang. The world seemed to be tranquil, the valley a haven of perfect peace. I saw not one gun, one item of the spoils which the bandits had brought back with them. The cooking-fires were still warm, but had been extinguished. The mud was still thick and deep and there was evidence of many horses having left the village fairly recently.

Perhaps the bandits had received intelligence of a large-scale counter-attack from General Liu's forces. Perhaps they had left to attack some new objective of their own. I determined to remain in the village for as long as possible in the hope that they would return.

I made a desultory perambulation of the village. I explored each of the remaining houses; I went for a walk along the main road out of the place. I walked back. There was no evidence for my first theory, that the village had been about to suffer an attack.

By lunchtime I was feeling pretty hungry and I returned to the house to pick at the cold remains of last night's supper. I helped myself to a glass of the missionary's excellent Madeira. I explored the anterooms of the ground floor and then went upstairs, determined, completely against my normal instincts, to investigate every room.

The bedroom next to mine still bore a faint smell of feminine perfume and was plainly Una Persson's. There was a mirror on the wall, a bottle of eau-de-Cologne beside the sleeping-mat, a few wisps of dark hair in an ivory hairbrush on the floor near the mirror. Otherwise, the room was furnished as barely as the others. I noticed a small inlaid table near a window leading onto a small balcony which overlooked the ruins of the village. There was a bulky package lying on the table, wrapped in oilskin, tied with cord.

As I passed it on my way to look out of the window I glanced at the package. And then I gave it very much of a second glance, for I had recognized my own name written in faded brown ink on yellow paper! Just the word "Moorcock". I did not know the handwriting, but I felt fully justified in tearing off the wrappings to reveal a great heap of closely written foolscap pages.

It was the manuscript which you, its rediscoverer (for I have no intention of making a fool of myself again), are about to read.

There was a note addressed to me from Bastable—brief and pointed—and the manuscript itself was in the same writing.

This must be, of course, what Una Persson had been referring to when she had told me that Bastable had left something of himself behind in the Valley of the Morning. I felt, too, that it was reasonable to surmise that she had meant to give the manuscript to me before she left (if she had actually known she was going to leave so suddenly).

I took the table, a stool and the manuscript onto the balcony, seating myself so that I was looking out over the mysteriously deserted village and the distant hills containing the valley I had sought for so long, and I settled down to read a story which was, if anything, stranger than the first Bastable had told me...

BOOK ONE

THE WORLD IN ANARCHY

CHAPTER ONE
The Return to Teku Benga

After I left you that morning, Moorcock, I had no intention of departing Rowe Island so hastily. I genuinely intended to do no more than take a stroll and clear my head. But I was very tired, as you know, and inclined to act impulsively. As I walked along the quayside I saw that a steamer was leaving; I observed an opportunity to stow away, did so, was undiscovered, and eventually reached the mainland of India, whereupon I made my way inland, got to Teku Benga (still hoping to get back to what I was convinced was my 'real' time), discovered that the way across remained impassable and considered the possibility of chucking myself off the cliff and having done with the whole mystery. But I hadn't the courage for that, nor the heart to go back to your world, Moorcock—that world that was so subtly different from the one I had originally left.

I suppose I must have gone into a decline of some sort (perhaps the shock, perhaps the sudden cessation of supplies of opium to my system, I don't know). I remained near the abyss separating me from what might have been the fountainhead of that particular knowledge I sought. I stared for hours at the dimly seen ruins of that ancient and squalid mountain fortress and I believe I must have prayed to it, begging it to release me from the awful fate it (or Sharan Kang, its dead priest-king) had condemned me to.

For some time (do not ask me how long) I lived the life of a wild beast, eating the small vermin I was able to trap, almost relishing the slow erosion of my mind and my civilized instincts.

When the snows came I was forced to look for shelter and was driven slowly down the mountainside until I discovered a cave which provided more than adequate shelter. The cave bore evidence that it had until recently been the lair of some wild beast, for there were many bones—of goats, wild sheep, hill dogs and the like (as well as the remains of more than one human being)—but there was no sign that its previous occupant was still in evidence. The cave was long and narrow, stretching so far back and becoming so dark that I never explored its whole extent and was content to establish myself close to the mouth, building no fire, but wrapping myself in the inadequately cured skins of my prey as the winter grew steadily colder.

The previous resident of the cave had been a huge tiger. I found this out one morning when I heard a peculiar snuffling noise and woke up to see the entrance blocked by a massive striped head and the beginnings of a pair of monstrous feline shoulders. The tiger regarded this cave as his winter home and plainly would not think much of the idea of sharing it equably with me. I leapt up and began to retreat into the depths of the cave, since my exit was completely blocked, as the tiger, who must have grown fatter during his summer in the lowlands, squeezed his way slowly in.

That was how I discovered the cave to be in actuality a tunnel—and moreover a man-made tunnel. It grew as dark as the grave as I continued my retreat along it. I steadied myself with my hands against the walls and slowly began to understand that the rough rock had given way to smooth and that the projections were, in fact, cunning carvings of a familiar pattern. I became a bit flustered, then—a bit mad. I remember giggling, then stopping myself, realizing that the tiger might still be behind me. I paused, feeling carefully on both sides of the narrow passage. I received a sickening sense of disgust as my groping fingers made out details of the carvings; my dizziness increased. And yet at the same time I was elated, knowing for certain that I had stumbled into one of Teku Benga's many secret corridors and that I might well have found my way back, at last, to that warren of passages which lay beneath the immeasurably ancient Temple of the Future Buddha! There was no question in my mind that, failing to find a way across the gorge, I had inadvertently discovered a way *under* it, for now the floor of the passage began to rise steeply and I was attacked by a coldness of a quality and intensity which was totally unlike the coldness of the natural winter. I had been terrified when I had first experienced it and I was terrified now, but my terror was mixed with hope. Strange little noises began to assail my ears, like the tinkling of temple bells, the whispering of a wind which carried half-formed words in an alien language. Once I had sought to escape all this, but now I ran towards it and I believe that I was weeping, calling out. And the floor of the passage seemed to sway as I ran on, the walls widened out so that I could no longer stretch my arms and touch them and at last, ahead of me, I saw a point of white light. It was the same I had seen before and I laughed. Even then I found my laughter harsh and mad, but I did not care. The light grew brighter and brighter until it was blinding me. Shapes moved behind the light; there were nameless, glowing colours; there were webs of some vibrating metallic substance and once more I was reminded of the legends of Hindu gods who had built machines to defy the laws of Space and Time.

And then I began to fall.

Head over heels I spun. It was as if I fell through the void which lies between the stars. Slowly all the little consciousness that remained had left me and I gave myself up to the ancient power which had seized me and made me its toy...

'm sorry if all this seems fanciful, Moorcock. You know that I'm not a particularly imaginative sort of chap. I began my maturity as an ordinary soldier, doing his duty to his country and his Empire. I should like nothing more than to continue my life in that vein, but fate had ordained otherwise. I awoke in darkness, desperately hoping that my flight through Time had been reversed and that I should discover myself back in my own age. There was no way of knowing, of course, for I was still in darkness, still in the tunnel, but the sounds had gone and that particular sort of coldness had gone. I got up, feeling my body in the hope that I'd discover I was wearing my old uniform, but I was not—I was still dressed in rags. This did not unduly concern me and I turned to retrace myself, feeling that if I was in the age I hoped to have left, then I would give myself up to the tiger and get it all over with.

At last I got back to the cave and there was no tiger. Moreover—and this improved my spirits—there was no sign that *I* had occupied the cave. I walked out into the snow and stood looking up at a hard, blue sky, taking great gulps of the thin air and grinning like a schoolboy, sure that I was 'home'.

My journey out of the mountains was not a pleasant one and how I ever escaped severe frostbite I shall never know. I passed through several villages and was treated with wary respect, as a holy man might be treated, and got warmer clothes and food, but none of those I spoke to could understand English and I had no familiarity with their dialect. Thus it was nearly a month before

I could begin to hope for confirmation of my belief that I had returned to my own time. A few landmarks began to turn up—a clump of trees, an oddly shaped rock, a small river—which I recognized and I knew I was close to the frontier station which Sharan Kang had attacked and thus been the cause of my first visit both to Teku Benga and, ultimately, the future.

The station came in sight a day or so later—merely a barracks surrounded by a few native brick huts and the whole enclosed by a serviceable wall. This was where our Native Police and their commanding officer had been killed and I admit that I prayed that I would find it as I had left it. There *were* signs of fighting and few signs of habitation and this cheered me up no end! I stumbled through the broken gateway of the little fort, hoping against hope that I would find the detachment of Punjabi Lancers and Ghoorkas I had left behind on my way to Kumbalari. Sure enough there were soldiers there. I shouted out in relief. I was weak from hunger and exhaustion and my voice must have sounded thinly through the warm spring air, but the soldiers sprang up, weapons at the ready, and it was only then that I realized they were white. Doubtless the Indian soldiers had been relieved by British.

Yet these men had recently been in a fight, that was clear. Had another band of Sharan Kang's men attacked the fort while I had been on my expedition into the old hill fox's territory?

I called out: "Are you British?"

I received the stout reply: "I certainly hope we are!"

And then I fell fainting on the dry dust of the compound.

CHAPTER TWO

The Dream — and the Nightmare — of the Chilean Wizard

Naturally enough, my first words on regaining consciousness, lying on a truckle bed in what remained of the barracks' dormitory, were:

"What's the year?"

"The *year*, sir?" The man who addressed me was a young, bright-looking chap. He had a sergeant's stripes on his dusty scarlet tunic (it was a Royal Londonderry uniform, a regiment having close connections with my own) and he held a tin cup of tea in one hand while the other was behind my head, trying to help me sit up.

"Please, sergeant, humour me, would you? What's the year?"

"It's 1904, sir."

So I had been 'lost' for two years. That would explain a great deal. I was relieved. Sipping the rather weak tea (I was later to discover it was almost their last) I introduced myself, giving my rank and my own regiment, telling the sergeant that I was, as far as I knew, the only survivor of a punitive expedition of a couple of years earlier—that I had been captured, escaped, wandered around for a bit and had only just managed to make it back. The sergeant accepted the story without any of the signs of suspicion which I had come to expect, but his next words alarmed me.

"So you would know nothing of the war, then, Captain Bastable?"

"A war? Here, on the Frontier? The Russians…"

"At the moment, sir, this is one of the few places scarcely touched by the war, though you are right in supposing that the Russians are amongst our enemies. The war is world-wide. Myself and less than a score of men are all that remains of the army which failed to defend Darjiling. The city and the best part of these territories are either under Russian control or the Russians have been, in turn, beaten by the Arabian Alliance. Personally I am hoping that the Russians are still in control. At least they let their prisoners live or, at worst, kill them swiftly. The last news we had was not good, however…"

"Are there no reinforcements coming from Britain?"

A look of pain filled the sergeant's eyes. "There will be little enough coming from Blighty for some time, I shouldn't wonder, sir. Most of Europe is in a far worse plight than Asia, having sustained the greatest concentration of bombs. The war is over in Europe, Captain Bastable. Here, it continues—a sort of alternative battle-ground, you might call it, with precious little for anyone to win. The power situation is grim enough— there's probably not one British keel capable of lifting, even if it exists…"

Now his words had become completely meaningless to me. I was aware of only one terrifying fact and I had become filled with despair: this world of 1904 bore even less relation to my own world than the one from which I had sought to escape. I begged the sergeant to explain recent history to me as he might explain it to a child, using my old excuse of partial amnesia. The man accepted the excuse and kindly gave me a breakdown of this world's history since the latter quarter of the nineteenth century. It was radically different either from your world, Moorcock or from the world of the future I described to you.

It appears that, by the 1870s, in Chile of all places, there had emerged the genius who had, in a few short years, been responsible for altering the lot of the world's poor, of providing plenty where once there had been famine, comfort where they had been only grinding misery. His name was Manuel O'Bean, the son of an Irish engineer who had settled in Chile and the Chilean heiress Esmé Piatnitski (perhaps the wealthiest woman in South or Central America). O'Bean had shown signs of an enormous capacity to learn and to invent at an extraordinarily young age. His father, needless to say, had encouraged him and O'Bean had learned everything his father could pass on by the time he was eight years old. With the resources made available by his mother's wealth, O'Bean had nothing to thwart this flowering of his mechanical genius. By the time he was twelve he had invented a whole new range of mining equipment which, when applied to his family's holdings, increased their wealth a hundred-fold. Not only did he have an enormous talent for planning and building new types of machine, he also had the ability to work out new power sources which were less wasteful and infinitely cheaper than the crude sources up to that time in use. He developed a method of converting and reconverting electricity so that it did not need to be carried through wires but could be transmitted by means of rays to almost anywhere in the world from any other point. His generators were small, efficient and required the minimum of power, and these in turn propelled most of the types of machinery he invented. Other engines, including sophisticated forms of steam-turbine depending on fast-heating liquids other than water, were also developed. As well as the mining and farming equipment he developed in those early years, O'Bean (still less than fifteen years old) invented a collection of highly efficient war-machines (he was still a boy and was fascinated, as boys are, with such things), including underwater boats, mobile cannons, airships (in collaboration with the great flying expert, the Frenchman La Perez) and self-propelled armoured carriages sometimes called "land ironclads". However, O'Bean soon abandoned this line of research as his social conscience developed. By the time he was eighteen he had sworn never to put his genius to war-like purposes again and instead concentrated on machines which would irrigate deserts, tame forests, and turn the whole world into an infinitely rich garden which would feed the hungry and thus extinguish what he believed to be the wellspring of most human strife.

By the beginnings of the new century, therefore, it seemed that Utopia had been achieved. There was not one person in the world who was not well-nourished and did not have the opportunity to receive a good education. Poverty had been abolished almost overnight.

Man *can* live by bread alone when all his energies are devoted to attaining that bread, but once his mind is clear, once he has ceased to labour through all his waking hours to find food, then he begins to think. If he has the opportunity to gather facts, if his mind is educated, then he begins to consider his position in the world and compare it with that of other men. Now it was possible for thousands to understand that the world's power was in the hands of a few—the landowners, the industrialists, the politicians and the ruling classes. All these people had welcomed O'Bean's scientific and technical advances—for they were able to lease his patents, to build their own machines, to make themselves richer as those they ruled became better off. But twenty-five years is enough time for a new generation to grow up—a generation which has never known dire poverty and which, unlike a previous generation, is no longer merely grateful that it has leisure time and more than enough to eat. That generation begins to want to control its own fate in myriad ways. In short, it seeks political power.

By 1900, in this world, civil strife had become a fact of life in almost every nation, large and small. In some countries, usually those which had been the most backward, revolutions succeeded, and, attended by a fanatical nationalism, new power groups were formed. The Great Powers found their colonial territories snatched from them—in Asia, in Africa, in the Americas—and since the sources of power were cheap and O'Bean's patents were distributed everywhere, since military power no longer depended so much on large, well-trained armies (or even navies), these older nations were wary of starting wars with the newer nations, preferring to try to retain their positions by means of complicated diplomacy, by building up 'spheres of influence'. But complicated diplomatic games played in the far corners of the world tend to have a habit of creating stronger tensions at home, so in Europe, in particular, but also in the United States and Japan, nationalism grew stronger and stronger and fierce battles of words began to take place between the Great Powers. Trade embargoes, crippling and unnecessarily unfair tariff restrictions were applied and returned. A madness began to fill the heads of those who ruled. They saw themselves threatened from within by their young people, who demanded what they saw as more social justice, and from without by their neighbouring countries. More and more resources were devoted to the building up of land, sea and air fleets, of large guns, of armies which could control dissident populations (and at the same time, hopefully, absorb them). In many countries enforced military service, after the Prussian model, became the norm— and this in turn brought an increasingly furious reaction from those who sought to reform their governments. Active, violent revolutionary methods began to be justified by those who had originally hoped to achieve their ends by means of oratory and the ballot box.

What O'Bean himself thought of this nobody knows, but it was likely that he did feel enormously guilty. One story has it that on the inevitable day when the Great Powers went to war he quietly committed suicide.

The war was at first contained only in Europe, and in the first weeks most of the major cities of the Continent and Britain were reduced to ash and rubble. A short-lived Central American Alliance lasted long enough to go to war with the United States and quickly achieved a similar end. Huge mobile war machines rolled across the wasted land; sinister aerial battleships cruised smoke-filled skies; while under the water lurked squadrons of subaquatic men-o'-war, often destroying one another without ever once rising to the surface where more conventional ironclads blasted rivals to bits with the horrifically powerful guns invented by a boy of thirteen years old.

"But most of the *real* fighting's over now," said the sergeant, with a tinge of contempt. "The fuel ran out for the generators and the engines. The war machines that were left just—well— stopped. It all went back to cavalry and infantry and that sort of stuff for a while, but there was hardly anyone knew *how* to fight like that—and precious few people left to do it. And not much ammunition, I shouldn't wonder. We're down to about one cartridge each." He tapped the weapon which hung at his belt. "It'll be bayonets, if we ever do meet the enemy. The bally Indians'll be top dogs—those who've still got swords and lances and bows and arrows and that…"

"You don't think the war will stop? People must be shocked by what's happened—sickened by it all."

The soldier shook his head, waxing philosophical. "It's a madness, sir. We've all got it. It could go on until the last human being crawls away from the body of the chap he's just bashed to bits with a stone. That's what war is, sir—madness. You don't think about what you're doing. You forget, don't you—you just go on killing and killing." He paused, almost embarrassed. "Leastways, that's what *I* think."

I conceded that he could well be right. Filled with unutterable gloom, obsessed by the irony of my escape from a relatively peaceful world into this one, I yet felt the need somehow to get back to England, to see for myself if the sergeant had told me the truth, or whether he had exaggerated, either from a misguided sense of drama, or from despair at his own position.

I told him that I should like to try to return to my own country, but he smiled pityingly at me, telling me that there wasn't the slightest chance. If I headed, say, for Darjiling, then I was bound to be captured by the Russians or the Arabians. Even if I managed to reach the coast, there were no ships in the harbours (if there were harbours!) or the aerodromes. My best plan, he suggested, was to fall in with them. They had done their duty and their position was hopeless. They planned to get up into the hills and make some sort of life for themselves there. The sergeant thought that, with the population killing itself off so rapidly, game would proliferate and we should be able to live by hunting—"and live pretty well, too". But I had had enough of the hills already. For better or worse, as soon as I had recovered my strength I would try to get to the coast.

A couple of days later I bid farewell to the sergeant and his men. They begged me not to be so foolhardy, that I was going to certain death.

"There was talk of plague, sir," said the sergeant. "Terrible diseases brought about by the collapse of the sanitary systems."

I listened politely to all the warnings and then, politely, ignored them.

Perhaps I had had my share of bad luck, for good luck

stayed with me for the rest of my journey across the Indian sub-
continent. Darjiling had, indeed, fallen to the Arabians, but they
had evacuated the shell of that city soon after occupying it. Their
forces were stretched pretty thin and had been needed on the
home front. There were still one or two divisions left, but they
were busy looking for Russians, and when they discovered that
I was English they took this to mean that I was a friend (towards
the end, I gathered, there had been some attempt to make a pact
between Britain and Arabia) and these chaps were under what
turned out to be the utterly false impression that we were fighting
on the same side. I fell in with them. They were heading for
Calcutta—or where Calcutta had once stood—where there was
some hope of getting a ship back to the Middle East. There was a
ship, too—a, to them, old-fashioned steamer, using coal-burning
engines—and although the name on its side was in Russian, it
flew the crossed-scimitar flag of the Arabian Alliance. It was in
a state of terrible disrepair and one took one's life in one's hands
when going aboard, but there had been a chance in a million of
finding any kind of ship and I was not in a mood to miss it. She
had been an old cargo ship and there was very little room, as such,
for passengers. Most of the men were crowded into the holds and
made as comfortable as possible. As an officer and a 'guest' I
got to share a cabin with four of the Arabians, three of whom
were Palestinians and one of whom was an Egyptian. They all
spoke perfect English and, while somewhat reserved, were decent
enough company, going so far as to lend me a captain's uniform
and most of the necessities of life which I had learned, in recent
months, to do without.

The ship made slow progress through the Bay of Bengal
and I relieved my boredom by telling my companions that I had
been the prisoner of a Himalayan tribe for several years and thus
getting them to fill in certain details of their world's history which
the sergeant had been unable to give me.

There was some talk of a man whom they called the "Black Attila", a leader who had emerged of late in Africa and whom they saw as a threat to themselves. Africa had not suffered as badly from the effects of the war as Europe and most of her nations—many only a few years old—had done their best to remain neutral. As a result they had flourishing crops, functioning harvesting machines and a reserve of military power with which to protect their wealth. The Black Attila had growing support in the Negro nations for a *jehad* against the whites (the Arabians were included in this category, as were Asiatics), but, at the last my informants had heard, was still consolidating local gains and had shown no sign of moving against what remained of the countries of the West. There were other rumours which said that he had already been killed, while some said he had invaded and conquered most of Europe.

The ship had no radio apparatus (another example of my good fortune, it emerged, for the Arabians had never reached the point of signing a pact with Britain!), and thus there was no means of confirming or denying these reports. We sailed down the coast of India, through the Gulf of Mannar, managed to take on coal at Agatti in the Laccadives, got into heavy weather in the Arabian Sea, lost three hands and most of our rigging, entered the Red Sea and were a few days away from the approach to the Suez Canal when, without any warning at all, the ship was struck by several powerful torpedoes and began to sink almost immediately.

It was the work of an undersea torpedo-boat—one of the few still functioning—and it was not, it emerged, an act of war at all, but an act of cynical piracy.

However, the pirate had done his work too well. The ship sighed, coughed, and went to the bottom with most of her passengers and crew. I and about a dozen others were left clinging to what little wreckage there was.

The undersea boat lifted its prow from the water for a few

seconds to observe its handiwork, saw that there was nothing to be gained by remaining, and left us to our fate. I suppose we should have been grateful that it did not use the guns mounted along its sides to finish us off. Ammunition had become scarce almost everywhere, it seemed.

CHAPTER THREE

The Polish Privateer

I shan't describe in detail my experiences of the next twenty-four hours. Suffice to say that they were pretty grim as I watched my companions sink, one by one, beneath the waves and knew that ultimately I should be joining them. I suppose I have had a great deal of practice in the art of survival and somehow I managed to remain afloat, clinging to my pathetic bit of flotsam, until the late afternoon of the next day when the monster rose from the waves, steaming water pouring off its blue-black skin, its great crystalline eyes glaring at me, and a horrible, deep-throated roaring issuing from its belly. At first my exhausted mind *did* see it as a living creature but my second thoughts were that the undersea torpedo-boat had returned to finish me off.

Slowly the disturbance in the water ceased and the growling subsided to a quiet purring and the sleek and slender craft came to rest on the surface. From hatches fore and aft sailors in sea-green uniforms sprang onto the deck and ran quickly to the rails. One of them flung a life-buoy out over the side and with the last of my strength I swam towards it, seizing it and allowing myself to be hauled towards the ship. Hands dragged me aboard and a cup of rum was forced down my throat while blankets were thrown around me and I was carried bodily along the rocking deck and down into the forward hatch. This hatch was closed swiftly over us and as I was borne below I could feel the ship itself descending back below the waves. The whole thing had taken place in the space of a few minutes and I had the impression of urgency, as if much had been risked in coming to the surface at all. I surmised that this could not be the same ship (it seemed larger, for one thing) which had left me to my fate, that it must be another. It was certainly not a British ship, and I could make little of the language spoken by the seamen who carried me to a small, steel-walled cabin and stripped me of my sodden Arabian uniform before lowering me into the bunk and drawing warm blankets over me. It was probably a Slavonic language and I wondered if I had been made a prisoner of war by the Russians. I heard the ship's engines start up again, and there was a barely perceptible lurch as we began to go forward at what I guessed to be pretty high speed. Then, careless of what my fate might be, I fell into a heavy and, thankfully, dreamless sleep.

Upon awakening, I glanced automatically towards the porthole but, of course, could not tell whether it was night or day, let alone what the time was! All I saw was dark green swirling water rushing past, faintly illuminated by the lights from the ship as it coursed with shark-like speed through the deeps. For a while I stared in fascination at the sight, hoping to make out some details of my first glimpse of the mysterious underwater world, but we were doubtless moving too rapidly. As I stared, the door of the cabin opened and a seaman entered, bearing a large tin cup which proved to contain hot, black coffee. He spoke in a thick accent:

"The captain's compliments, sir. Would you care to join him in his cabin, at your leisure."

I accepted the coffee, noting that my borrowed uniform had been washed, dried and pressed and that a fresh set of undergarments had been laid out on the small table fixed against the opposite wall to the bunk.

"Gladly," I replied. "Will there be someone to escort me there when I have completed my toilet and dressed?"

"I will wait outside for you, sir." The sailor saluted and left the cabin, closing the door smartly behind him. There was no question that this was a superbly disciplined ship—the efficiency with which I had been rescued spoke of that—and I hoped that the discipline extended to the honouring of the ordinary conventions of war!

As quickly as I could I readied myself and soon presented myself outside the cabin door. The sailor set off along the narrow, tubular passage which was remarkable for possessing cork catwalks positioned on sides and ceiling as well as floor, indicating that the ship was designed to function at any of the main positions of the quadrant. My surmise proved to be accurate (there were also 'decks' on the outside of the hull to match the catwalks, while the main control room was a perfect globe pivoting to match the angle of the ship—merely, it emerged, one of O'Bean's 'throwaway' ideas!) and the underwater craft was essentially much in advance of anything I had encountered in that other future of 1973.

The tubular passage led us to an intersection and we took the portside direction, climbed a small companionway and found ourselves outside a plain, circular steel door upon which the seaman knocked, uttering a few words in his unfamiliar language. A single word answered him from the other side of the door and he pulled back a recessed catch to open it and admit me, saluting again before he left.

I found myself in an almost familiar version of any captain's quarters of a ship of my own world. There was plenty of well-polished mahogany and brass, a few green plants in baskets hanging from ceilings and walls, a neatly made single bunk, a small chart-table on which were several maps and around the edges of which were clipped a variety of instruments. Framed prints of clipper-ships and of old charts were fixed to the walls. The lighting glowed softly from the whole ceiling and had the quality of daylight (yet another of O'Bean's casual inventions). A smallish, dapper figure, with whiskers trimmed in the Imperial style, rose to greet me, adjusting his cap on his head and smiling almost shyly. He was a young man, probably not much older that myself, but he had the lines of experience upon his face and his eyes were the eyes of a much older man—steady and clear, yet betraying a certain cool irony. He stretched out a hand and I shook it, finding the grip firm and not ungentle. There was something naggingly familiar about him, but my mind refused to accept the truth until, in good, but gutturally accented, English, he introduced himself:

"Welcome aboard the *Lola Montez*, captain. My name is Korzeniowski and I am her master."

I was too stunned to speak, for I was confronting a much younger version of my old mentor from the days I spent aboard *The Rover*. Then, Korzeniowski had been (or would be) a Polish airship captain. The implications of all this were frightening. Was there now a chance that I might meet a version of *myself* in this other world? I recovered my politeness. Plainly Korzeniowski knew nothing of me and I introduced myself, for better or worse, by my name and my real regiment, explaining quickly how I had come to be wearing my rather elaborate Arabian uniform. "I hope Poland is not at war with the Arabian Alliance," I added.

Captain Korzeniowski shrugged, turning towards a cabinet containing a number of bottles and glasses. "What will you have, Captain Bastable?"

"Whisky with a splash of soda, if you please. You are very kind."

Korzeniowski took out the whisky decanter, gesturing casually with it as he extracted a glass from the rack. "Poland is not at war with anyone now. First Germany broke her, then Russia extinguished her, then Russia herself ceased to exist, as a nation at least. Poor Poland. Her struggles are over for all time. Perhaps something less ill-fated will emerge from the ruins." He handed me a full glass, made as if to toss off his own, in the Polish manner, then restrained himself and sipped it almost primly, tugging at the lobe of his left ear, seeming to reprove himself for having been about to make a flamboyant gesture.

"But you and your crew are Polish," I said. "The ship is Polish."

"We belong to no nation now, though Poland was the birthplace of most of us. The ship was once the finest in our navy. Now it is the last survivor of the fleet. We have become what you might call 'privateers'. It is how we survive during the apocalypse." His eyes held a hint of sardonic pride. "I think we are rather good at it—though the prey becomes scarce. We had our eye on your ship for a while, but it did not seem worth the waste of a torpedo. You might be glad to know that the ship which attacked you was called the *Mannanan* and that she belonged to the Irish navy."

"*Irish?*" I was surprised. Home Rule, then, was a fact in this world.

"We could not stop to pick you up right away, but decided that you would have to take your chances. The *Mannanan* was a well-equipped ship and we were able to wound her and force her to the surface quite easily. She was a 'fine prize', as the buccaneers would say!" He laughed. "We were able to take stores aboard which will keep us going for three months. And spare parts."

She had deserved whatever Captain Korzeniowski had done to her. Doubtless he had shown more mercy in his treatment of the *Mannanan* than she had shown to our poor, battered steamer. But I could not bring myself to voice these sentiments aloud and thus condone what had been, after all, a similar act of piracy on the part of the *Lola Montez*.

"Well, Captain Bastable," said Korzeniowski, lighting a thick cheroot and signaling for me to help myself from his humidor, "what do you want us to do with you? It's normally our habit to put survivors off at the nearest land and let them take their chances. But yours is something of a special case. We're making for the Outer Hebrides, where we have a station. Is there anywhere between here and there that we can put you off? Not that there is anywhere particularly habitable on land, these days."

I told him how I planned to try to reach England and that if there was any chance of being put off on the South Coast I would more than welcome it. He raised his eyebrows at this.

"If you had said Scotland I might have understood—but the South Coast! Having been the agent of your escape from death, I am not sure I could justify to my conscience my becoming the instrument of your destruction! Have you not heard? Have you any idea of the hell which Southern England has become?"

"I gather that London sustained some very heavy bombing…"

Evidently Korzeniowski could not restrain a bleak smile at this. "I have always appreciated British understatement," he told me. "What else have you gathered?"

"That there is a risk of catching disease—typhus, cholera, and so on."

"And so on, yes. Do you know what *kind* of bombs the air fleets were dropping towards the end, Captain Bastable?"

"Pretty powerful ones, I should imagine."

"Oh, extremely. But they were not explosive—they were bacteria. The bombs contained different varieties of plague, captain. They had a lot of scientific names, but they soon became known by their nicknames. Have you seen, for instance, the effects of the Devil's Mushroom?"

"I haven't heard of it."

"It is called by that name after the fungus which begins to form on the surface of the flesh less than two hours after the germs have infected the victim. Scrape off the fungus and the flesh comes away with it. In two days you look like one of those rotten trees you might have seen in a forest sometimes, but happily by that time you are quite dead and you have no pain at all. Then there's Prussian Emma, which causes haemorrhaging from all orifices—*that* death is singularly painful, I'm told. And there's Eye Rot, Red Blotch, Brighton Blight. Quaint names, aren't they? As colourful as the manifestations of the diseases on the skin. Aside from the diseases, there are roving gangs of cut-throats warring on one another and killing any other human being they find (not always prettily). From time to time you might set foot on a gas bomb which is triggered as you step on it and blows a poison gas up into your face. If you escape those dangers, there are a dozen more. Believe me, Captain Bastable, the only clean life now—the only life for a man—is on the high seas (or under them). It is to the sea that many of us have returned, living out our lives by preying upon one another, admittedly. But it is an existence infinitely preferable to the terrors and degradations of the land. And one still has a certain amount of freedom, is still somewhat in control of one's own fate. Dry land is what the medieval painters imagined Hell to be. Give me the purgatory of the sea!"

"I am sure I would agree with you," I told him, "but I would still see it for myself."

Korzeniowski shrugged. "Very well. We'll put you off at

Dover, if you like. But if you should change your mind, I could use a trained officer, albeit an army officer, aboard this vessel. You could serve with me."

This was indeed a case of history repeating itself (or was it prefiguring itself?). Korzeniowski did not know it, but I had already served with him—and not in the army either, but in airships. It would be second nature for me to sail with him now. But I thanked him and told him that my mind was made up.

"Nonetheless," he said, "I'll leave the berth open to you for a bit. You never know."

A few days later I was put ashore on a beach just below the familiar white cliffs of Dover and waved goodbye to the *Lola Montez* as she sank below the surface of the waves and was gone. Then I shouldered my knapsack of provisions, took a firm grip on the fast-firing carbine I had been given, and turned my steps inland, towards London.

CHAPTER FOUR

The King of East Grinstead

If I had considered Korzeniowski's description of post-war England to be fanciful, I soon had cause to realize that he had probably restrained himself when painting a picture of the conditions to be found there. Plague was, indeed, widespread, and its victims were to be seen everywhere. But the worst of the plagues were over, largely because most of the population remaining had been killed off by them and those who survived were resistant to most of the strains—or had somehow recovered from them. Those who *had* recovered were sometimes missing a limb, or a nose, or an eye, while others had had parts of their faces or bodies eaten away altogether. I observed several bands of these poor, half-rotted creatures, in the ruins of Dover and Canterbury, as I made my way cautiously towards London.

The inhabitants of the Home Counties had descended from the heights of civilization to the depths of barbarism in a few short years. The remains of the fine towns, the clean, broad highways, the monorail systems, the light, airy architecture of the world O'Bean had created, were still there to speak of the beauty that had come and gone so swiftly, but now bands of beast-men camped in them, tore them down to make crude weapons and primitive shelters, hunted each other to death among them. No woman was safe and, among certain of the 'tribes' roving the ruins, children were regarded as particularly excellent eating! Former bank managers, members of the stock exchange, respectable tradesmen, had come to regard vermin as delicacies and were prepared to tear a man's jugular from his throat with their teeth if it would gain them the possession of a dead cat. Few modern weapons were in evidence (the production of rifles and pistols had been on the decline since the invention of airships and subaquatic boats), but rudely made spears, bows and arrows, knives and pikes could be found in almost every hand. By day I lay hidden wherever there was good cover, watching the savages go by, and I traveled at night, risking ambush, since I regarded my chances as being better at night when most of the 'tribesmen' returned to their camps. The country had not only sustained the most horrifying mass aerial bombardment, but had also (in this area in particular) received huge punishment from long-range guns firing from across the Channel. Twice the Home Counties had been invaded by forces coming from sea and air, and these had ravaged what remained, taking the last of the food, blowing up those buildings which still stood, before being driven back by the vestiges of our army. At night the hills of Kent and Surrey sparkled with points of light indicating the locations of semi-nomadic camps where huge fires burned day and night. The fires were not merely there for cooking and heating, but to burn the regular supply of plague-created corpses.

And so my luck held until I reached the outskirts of East Grinstead, once a pretty little village which I had known well as a boy, but now a wasteland of blasted vegetation and torn masonry. As usual I inspected the place from cover, noting the presence of what seemed to be a crudely made stockade of tree-trunks near the northernmost end of the village. From this armed men came and went regularly, and I was surprised to see that many of them carried rifles and shotguns and were dressed in rather more adequate rags than the people I had seen to date. The community itself seemed to be a larger one than the others, and better organized, settled in one place rather than roaming about a small area of countryside. I heard the distinctive sounds of cattle, sheep and goats and surmised that a few of these animals had survived and were being kept for safety inside the stockade. Here was 'civilization' indeed! I considered the possibility of making my presence known and seeking aid from the inhabitants, who might be expected to behave in a somewhat less aggressive manner than the people I had observed up to now. But, warily, I continued to keep watch on the settlement and see what information I could gather before I revealed myself.

It was a couple of hours later that I had reason to congratulate myself on my caution. I had hidden in a small brick building which had somehow survived the bombing. It had been used, I think, as a woodstore and was barely large enough to admit me. A grille, designed for ventilation, was the means by which I could look out at the stockade without being seen. Three men, dressed in a miscellaneous selection of clothing which included a black bowler hat, a deerstalker and a panama, a woman's fur cape, golfing trousers, a leather shooting-coat, a tailcoat and an opera cloak, were escorting a prisoner back along the path to the gate. The prisoner was a young woman, tall and dressed in a long black military topcoat which had evidently been tailored for her. She had a black divided skirt and black riding-boots and there was no question in my mind that she, like me, was some sort of interloper. They were treating her roughly, pushing her so that she fell over twice and struggled to her feet only with the greatest difficulty (her hands were tied behind her back). There was something familiar about her bearing, but it was only when she turned her head to speak to one of her captors (evidently speaking with the greatest contempt, for the man struck her in the mouth by way of reply) that I recognized her. It was Mrs. Persson, the revolutionist whom I had first met on Captain Korzeniowski's airship, *The Rover*, and whom I understood to be Korzeniowski's daughter. That could not be true now, for this woman was approximately the same age as Korzeniowski. I had had enough of speculating about the mysteries and paradoxes of Time—they were beginning to become familiar to me and I was learning to accept them as one might accept the ordinary facts of human existence, without question. Now I merely saw Una Persson as a woman who was in danger and who must therefore be rescued. I had my carbine and several magazines of ammunition and I had the advantage that none of the inhabitants of the stockade was aware of my presence. I waited for nightfall and then crept out of my hiding-place, thanking Providence that the full moon was hidden behind thick cloud.

I got to the stockade and saw that it was an extremely crude affair—no savage would have owned to its manufacture—and easily scaled, so long as the timber did not collapse under me. Slowly I climbed to the top and got my first sight of the interior.

It was a scene of the utmost barbarity. Una Persson hung spreadeagled and suspended on a kind of trellis in the centre of the compound. In front of her, cross-legged, sat what must have been the best part of the 'tribe'—many of them bearing the deformities marking them as recipients of various plague viruses. Behind the scaffold was a sort of dais made from a large oak refectory table, and on the table there had been placed a high-backed, ornately carved armchair of the sort which our Victorian ancestors regarded as the very epitome of 'Gothic' good taste. The velvet of the chair was much torn and stained and the woodwork had been covered with some sort of poorly applied gold lacquer. A number of fairly large fires blazed in a semi-circle behind the dais and oily smoke drifted across the scene, while the red flames leapt about like so many devils and were reflected in the sweating faces of the gathered inhabitants of the stockade. This was what I saw before I dropped to the other side of the fence and crept into the shadow of one of the ramshackle shelters clustered nearby.

A sort of hideous crooning now issued from the throats of the onlookers, and they swayed slowly from side to side, their eyes fixed on Una Persson's half-naked body. Una Persson herself did not struggle, but remained perfectly still in her bonds, staring back at them with an expression of utter disgust and contempt. As I had admired it once before, again I admired her courage. Few of us, in her position, could have behaved so well.

Since she did not seem to be in any immediate danger, I waited to see what would next develop.

From a hut larger than the rest and set back behind the semi-circle of fires, there now emerged a tall and corpulent figure dressed in full morning-dress, with a fine grey silk hat at a jaunty angle on his head, his right thumb stuck in the pocket of his waistcoat, a diamond pin in his cravat, looking for all the world like some music-hall performer of my own time. Slowly, with an air of insouciance, he ascended the dais and seated himself with great self-importance in his gold chair while the crowd ceased its humming and swaying for a moment to greet him with a monstrous shout whose words I could not catch.

His own voice was clear enough. It was reedy and yet brutal and, for all that it was the uneducated voice of a small shopkeeper, it carried authority.

"Loyal subjects of East Grinstead," it began. "The man—or woman—who pulls their weight is welcome here as you well know. But East Grinstead has never taken kindly to foreigners, scroungers, Jews and loafers, as is also well known. East Grinstead knows how to deal with 'em. We have our traditions. Now this here interloper, this spy, was caught hanging round near East Grinstead obviously up to no good—and also, I might add, armed to the teeth. Well, draw your own conclusions, my subjects. There is not much doubt in my—our—mind that she is by way of being a definite foreign aviator, probably come back to see how we are getting on here after all them bombs she dropped on us did their damage. She has found a flourishing community—bloody but unbowed and ready for anything. Given half a chance, I shouldn't be surprised if she was about to report back to her compatriots that East Grinstead wasn't finished—not by a long shot finished—and we could have expected another lot of bombs. But," and his voice dropped and became ruthless and sinister, plainly relishing Una's pain, "she won't *be* going back. And we're going to teach her a lesson, aren't we, about what foreign aviators and spies can expect if they try it on over East Grinstead and Major John!"

He continued in this vein and I listened in horror. Could this man once have served behind a counter in an ordinary suburban shop? Perhaps he had served me with an ounce of licorice or a packet of tea. And his 'subjects', who growled and giggled and trembled with blood-lust, were these once the decent, conservative folk of the Home Counties? Did it take so little time to strip them of all their apparent civilization? If ever I returned to my own world I would look on these people in a new light.

King John of East Grinstead had risen from his chair and someone had handed him a brand. The firelight turned his grey, unshaven face into the mask of a devil as he raised the brand above his head, his eyes glowing and his lips drawn back in a bestial grin.

"*Now* we'll teach her!" he yelled. And his subjects rose up, arms extended, screaming to him to do what he was about to do.

The brand came down and began to extend towards Una Persson's head. She could not see what was happening, but it was obvious that she guessed. She struggled once in the ropes, then her lips came firmly together and she closed her eyes as the brand moved closer towards her.

Scarcely thinking, I raised my carbine to my shoulder, took aim, and shot Major John, the King of East Grinstead, squarely between the eyes. His face was almost comic in its astonishment and then the great bulk fell forward off the dais and lay in a heap before its stunned subjects.

I moved quickly then, thankful for my army training.

While those hideously ravaged faces looked at me with expressions of horror, I ran to the trellis and with a few quick strokes of my knife cut Una Persson free.

Then, quite deliberately, I shot down three of the nearest men. One of them had been armed and I signed to Una Persson to pick up the rifle, which she did as quickly as she could, though she was plainly suffering a good deal of pain.

"This place is surrounded by men," I told them. "All are crack shots. The first to threaten us with his weapon will die as swiftly as your leader. As you can see, we are merciless. If you remain within the stockade and allow us to go through the gate unhampered, no more of you will be harmed."

A few of the people growled like animals, but were too nonplused and alarmed to do anything more. I could not resist a parting speech as we got to the gate.

"I might tell you that I am British," I said. "As British as you are and from the same part of the world. And I am disgusted by what I see. This is no way for Britons to behave. Remember your old standards. Recall what they once meant to you. The fields remain and you have stock. Grow your food as you have always grown it. Breed the beasts. Build East Grinstead into a decent place again…"

Una Persson put a hand on my arm, whispering: "There is not much time. They'll soon realize that you have no men. They are already beginning to look for them and not see them. Come, we'll make for my machine."

We backed out of the gate and closed it behind us. Then, bent low, we began to run. I followed Una Persson and she plainly had a good idea of where she was going. We ran through a wood and across several overgrown fields, into another wood, and here we paused, listening for sounds of pursuit, but there was none.

Panting, Una Persson pushed on until the forest thinned. Then she bent over a bush and without any apparent effort seemed to pull the whole thing up by the roots, revealing the faint gleam of metal. She operated a control, there was a buzz and a hatch swung upwards.

"Get in," she said, "there's just about room for both of us."

I obeyed. I found myself in a cramped chamber, surrounded by a variety of unfamiliar instruments. Una Persson closed the hatch over her head and began turning dials and flicking switches until the whole machine was shaking and whining. She peered through a contraption which looked to me rather like a stereoscopic viewer, then pulled a large lever right back. The whining sound increased its pitch and the machine began to move—heading downwards into the very bowels of the earth.

"What sort of machine is this?" I enquired in my amazement.

"Haven't you seen one before?" she said casually. "It's an O'Bean Mark Five tunneler. It's about the only way to move these days without being spotted. It's slow. But it's sure." She smiled, pausing in her inspection of the controls to offer me her hand. "I haven't thanked you. I don't know who you are, sir, but I'm very grateful for what you did. My mission in this part of Britain is vital and now it has some chance of success."

It had become extremely hot and I fancied that we were nearing the core of the planet!

"Not at all," I replied. "Glad to be of service. My name's Bastable. You're Mrs. Persson, aren't you?"

"Una Persson," she said. "Were you sent to help me, then?"

"I happened to be passing, that was all." I wished now that I hadn't admitted to knowing her name—the explanation could

prove embarrassing. I made a wild guess, remembering something
of what I had been told about her when I flew with *The Rover*. "I
recognized your photograph. You were an actress, weren't you?"

She smiled, wiping the perspiration from her face with a
large, white handkerchief. "Some would say that I still am."

"What sort of depth are we at?" I asked, feeling quite faint now.

"Oh, no more than a hundred feet. The air system isn't working
properly and I don't know enough about these metal moles to fix
it. I don't think we're in any immediate danger, however."

"How did you come to be in East Grinstead, Mrs. Persson?"

She did not hear me above the shaking of the machine and the
weird whining of its engine. She made some sort of adjustment to
our course as she cupped her hand to her ear and made me repeat
the question.

She shrugged. "What I was looking for was nearby. There
was some attempt to set up a secret centre of government towards
the end. There were plans for an O'Bean machine which was
never perfected. There is only one of its type—in Africa. The
plans will clarify one or two problems which were troubling us."

"In Africa! You have come from Africa?"

"Yes. Ah, here we are." She pushed two levers forward and I
felt the tunneling machine begin to tilt, rising towards the surface.
"The ground must have been mainly clay. We've made good speed."

She cut off the engines, took one last glance into the viewer,
seemed satisfied, moved to the hatch, pressed a button. The hatch
opened, letting in the refreshing night air.

"You'd better get out first," she said.

I clambered thankfully from the machine, waiting for my
vision to adjust itself. The ground all around me was flat and
even. I could just make out the silhouette of what at first appeared
to be buildings arranged in a circle which enclosed us. There was
something decidedly familiar about the place. "Where are we?"
I asked her.

"I think it used to be called The Oval," she told me as she joined me on the grass. "Hurry up, Mr. Bastable. My airboat should be just over here."

It was a ridiculous emotion to feel at the time, I know, but I could not help experiencing a tinge of genuine shock at our having desecrated one of the most famous cricket pitches in the world!

CHAPTER FIVE

The Start of a New Career

Una Persson's Airboat was very different from the sort of aircraft I had become used to in the world of 1973. This was a flimsy affair consisting of an aluminium hull from which projected a sort of mast on which was mounted a large, three-bladed propeller. At the tail was a rudder, and on either side of the rudder were two small propellers. From the hull sprouted two broad, stubby fins which, like the small propellers, helped to stabilize and to steer the boat once it had taken to the air. We rose, swaying slightly, from the ground, while the boat's motor gave out a barely heard purring. It was only now that I sought to enquire of our destination. We were flying at about a height of one thousand feet over the remains of Inner London. There was not a landmark left standing. The entire city had been flattened by the invader's bombs. The legendary vengeance of Rome upon Carthage was as nothing compared to this. What had possessed one group of human beings to do such a thing to another? Was this, I wondered, how Hiroshima had looked after the *Shantien* had dropped her cargo of death? If so, I had much on my conscience. Or had I? I had begun to wonder if I moved from dream to dream. Was reality only what I made of it? Was there, after all, any such thing as 'history'?

"Where are we headed for, Mrs. Persson?" I asked, as we left London behind.

"My first stop will have to be in Kerry, where I have a refueling base."

"Ireland." I remembered the first subaquatic vessel I had seen. "I had hoped…"

I realized, then, that I had already made up my mind to accept Korzeniowski's offer. I had seen enough of my homeland and what its inhabitants had become. Korzeniowski's statements about the sea being the only "clean" place to be were beginning to make sense to me.

"Yes?" She turned. "I would take you all the way with me, Mr. Bastable. I owe you that, really. But I have scarcely enough power to get myself back and another passenger would make a crucial difference. Secondly you would probably have no taste for the kind of life I would take you to. I could drop you somewhere less dangerous than Southern England. It is the best I can offer."

"I was thinking of making for Scotland," I said. "Would I stand a better chance of survival there?" I was reluctant to disclose my actual destination. Korzeniowski would not appreciate my revealing his secret station.

She frowned. "The coast of Lancashire is about the best I can suggest. Somewhere beyond Liverpool. If you avoid the large cities, such as Glasgow, you should be all right. The Highlands themselves sustained very little bombing and I doubt if the plagues reached there."

And so it was that I bid farewell to Una Persson on a wild stretch of saltings beside the coast of Morecambe Bay near a village called Silverdale. It was dawn and the scenery around me made a welcome change from that I had so recently left. The air was full of the cries of sea-birds searching for their breakfast and a few sheep grazed on the salt-flats, taking a wary interest in me as they cropped the rich grass. In the distance was the sea, wide, flat and gleaming in the light of the rising sun. It was a comforting picture of rural tranquility and much more the England I had hoped to find when I had first landed at Dover. I waved goodbye to Mrs. Persson, watching her airboat rise rapidly into the sky and then swing away over the ocean, heading towards Ireland, then I shouldered my carbine and tramped towards the village.

The village was quite a large one, consisting mainly of those fine, stone houses one finds in such parts, but it was completely deserted. Either the inhabitants had fled under the threat of some supposed invasion, or else they had died of the plague and been buried by survivors who, in turn, had prudently gone away from the source of the disease. But there were no signs of any sort of disaster. Hoping to find food, maps and the like, I searched several houses, finding them completely in order. Much of the furniture had been neatly draped with dust-covers and all perishable food had been removed, but I was able to discover a good quantity of canned meats and bottled fruit and vegetables which, while heavy to carry, would sustain me for some time. I was also fortunate enough to find several good-quality maps of Northern England and Scotland. After resting for a day in Silverdale and granting myself the luxury of sleeping in a soft bed, I set off in the general direction of the Lake District.

I soon discovered that life was continuing at a fairly normal pace in these parts. The farming is largely sheep, and while the people who remained were forced to live in what was comparative poverty, the war had hardly altered their familiar pattern of existence. Instead of being regarded with fear and suspicion, as I had been in the Home Counties, I was welcomed, given food, and asked for any news I might have about the fate of the South. I was happy to tell all I knew, and to warn these friendly Northerners to beware of the insanity which had swept the counties around London. I was told that similar conditions existed near Birmingham, Manchester, Liverpool and Leeds, and I was advised to skirt Carlisle, if I could, for while the survivors of that city had not descended to the level of barbarism I had experienced in East Grinstead, they were still highly suspicious of those who seemed better off than themselves and there had been minor outbreaks of a variant of the disease known as Devil's Mushroom, which had not improved their disposition towards those who were not local to the area.

Heeding such warnings, proceeding with caution, taking advantage of what hospitality I was offered, I slowly made my way north, while the autumn weather—perhaps the finest I had ever known—lasted. I was desperate to get to the Islands before winter set in and the mountains became impassable. The Grampians, those stately monarchs of the Western Highlands, were reached, and at length I found myself crossing the great Rannoch Moor, heading in the general direction of Fort William, which lay under the shadow of Ben Nevis. The mountains shone like red Celtic gold in the clear sunshine of the early winter; there is no sight like it in the whole world and it is impossible to think of the British Isles as being in any way small, as they are in comparison with most other land areas, when you see the Grampians stretching in all directions, inhabited by nothing save the tawny Highland cattle, grouse and pheasant, their wild rivers full of trout and salmon. I ate like a king during that part of my journey—venison became a staple—and I was tempted to forget about my plan for joining Korzeniowski in the Outer Hebrides and to make my life here, taking over some abandoned croft, tending sheep, and letting the rest of the world go to perdition in any way it chose. But I knew that the winters could be harsh and I heard rumours that the old clans were beginning to re-form and that they were riding out on cattle-raids just as they had done in the days before the dreams of that drunken dandy Prince Charles Edward Stuart had brought the old Highland ways of life to a final and bitter end.

So I continued towards Skye, where I hoped I might find some sort of ferry still operating on the Kyle of Lochalsh. Sure enough, the inhabitants of Skye had not abandoned their crucial links with the mainland. Sailing boats plied a regular trade with the island and a haunch of venison bought me a passage on one of them just as the first snows of the winter started to drift from out of vast and steely skies.

My real difficulties then began! The people of Skye are not unfriendly. Indeed, I found them among the most agreeable folk in the world. But they are close-mouthed at the best of times, and my enquiries as to the possible whereabouts of an underwater vessel called the *Lola Montez* fell on deaf, if polite, ears. I could not gain an ounce of information. I was fed, given a considerable quantity of strong, mellow local whisky, invited to dances all over the island (I think I was regarded as an eligible bachelor by many of the mothers!) and allowed to help with any work which needed to be done. It was only when I offered to go out with the fishing-boats (hoping thus to spot Korzeniowski's ship) that my help was refused. From Ardvasar in the south to Kilmaluag in the north the story was the same—no-one denied that underwater boats called, from time to time, at the Islands, and no-one admitted it either. A peculiar, distant expression would come over the faces of young and old, male or female, whenever I broached the subject. They would smile, they would nod, they would purse their lips and they would look vaguely into the middle distance, changing the subject as soon as possible. I began to believe that not only was there at least one fueling station in the Outer Hebrides but that the islanders derived a good deal of their wealth, and therefore their security in troubled times, from the ship or ships which used such a station. It was not that they mistrusted me, but they saw no point in giving away information which could change their situation. At least, that is what I surmised.

Not that this made any great difference to me, it emerged. It was evident that an effort was made to help, that the fueling station was contacted and that my description and name were registered there, for one night, just after the spectacular New Year celebrations for which the Island folk are justly famous, I sat in a comfortable chair before a roaring fire in an excellent public house serving the township of Uig, sipping good malt whisky and chatting on parochial subjects, when the door of the hostelry opened, the wind howled in, bearing a few flakes of snow with it, until the door was slammed back in its face, and there, swathed in a heavy leather sea-cloak, stood my old friend Captain Josef Korzeniowski, bowing his stiff, Polish bow, and clicking the heels of his boots smartly together as he saluted me, his intelligent eyes full of sardonic amusement.

He was evidently well known to the regular customers of the inn and was greeted with warmth by several of them. I learned later that it was the captain's policy to share at least half of his booty with the islanders, and in return he received their friendship and their loyalty. When he needed new crew members, he recruited them from Skye, Harris, Lewis, North and South Uist and the smaller islands, for many had been professional seamen and, as Korzeniowski informed me, were among the most loyal, courageous and resourceful in the world, taking naturally to the dangers and the romance of his piratical activities!

We talked for hours, that night. I told him of my adventures and confirmed all he had said of what I would find in the South. In turn, he described some of his recent engagements and brought me up to date with what he knew of events in the rest of the world. Things had, if anything, gone from bad to worse. The whole of Europe and Russia had reverted almost completely to barbarism.

Things were scarcely any better in North America. Most of the nations which had remained neutral were internally divided and took no interest in international problems. In Africa the infamous Black Attila had swept through the entire Middle East and incorporated it into his so-called "Empire", had crossed the Mediterranean and claimed large areas of Europe, had conquered the best part of Asia Minor.

"There is even a story that he has designs on Britain and the United States," Korzeniowski informed me. "The only potential threat to his dreams of conquest would be the Australasian-Japanese Federation, but they pursue a policy of strict isolationism, refusing to become involved in any affairs but their own. It saved them from the worst effects of the war and they have no reason to risk losing everything by taking part in what they see as a conflict between different tribes of barbarians. The Black Attila has so far offered the A.J.F. no direct threat. Until he does, they will not move to stop him. The African nations who have so far been reluctant to join him are too weak to oppose him directly and are hopeful that if they do not anger him he will continue to concentrate on conquering territory which is, after all, already lost to civilization."

"But it is in the nature of such conquerors to consolidate easy gains before turning their attention on more powerful prey, is it not?" I said.

Korzeniowski shrugged and lit a pipe. The rest of the customers had long since gone home, and we sat beside a dying fire, the remains of a bottle of whisky between us. "Perhaps his impetus will dissipate itself eventually. It is what most people hope. So far he has brought some kind of order to the nations he has conquered—even a form of justice exists, crude though it is, for those with brown, black or yellow skins. The whites, I gather, receive a generally rawer deal. He has a consuming hatred for the Caucasian races, regarding them as the source of the world's evils—though I have heard that he has some white engineers in his employ. Presumably they are useful to him and would prefer to serve him rather than be subjected to some of the awful tortures he has devised for other whites. As a result, his resources grow. He has great fleets of land ironclads, airships, undersea dreadnoughts—and they are increasing all the time as he captures the remnants of the world's fighting machines."

"But what interest could he have in conquering England?" I asked. "There is nothing for him here."

"Only the opportunities for revenge," said the Polish sea-captain quietly. He looked at his watch. "It is high time I returned to my ship. Are you coming with me, Bastable?"

"That was my reason for being here," I said. I had a heavy heart as I digested the implications of all Korzeniowski had told me, but I tried to joke, remarking: "I used to dream of such things, as a boy. But now the dream is reality—I am about to serve under the Jolly Roger. Will it be necessary to sign my articles in blood?"

Korzeniowski clapped me on the shoulder. "It will not even be required of you, my dear fellow, to toast the Devil in grog—unless, of course, you wish to!"

I got my few possessions from my room and followed my new commander out into the chilly night.

CHAPTER SIX

"A Haven of Civilization"

For well over a year I sailed with Captain Korzeniowski aboard the *Lola Montez*, taking part in activities which would have carried the death sentence in many countries of my own world, living the desperate, dangerous and not always humane life of a latter-day sea wolf. In my own mind, if not in the minds of my comrades, I had become a criminal, and while my conscience still sometimes troubled me, I am forced to admit that I grew to enjoy the life. We went for the big game of the seas, never taking on an unarmed ship, and, by the logic which had come to possess this cruel and ravaged world, usually doing battle with craft who had as much to answer for in the name of piracy as had we.

But as the year progressed, and we roamed the seas of the world (ever cautious not to offend either the ships of the Australasian-Japanese Federation or those sailing under the colours of the Black Attila), we found our prey becoming increasingly scarce. As sources of fuel ran out or parts needed replacing, even the few ships which had survived the war began to disappear. I felt something of the emotions that an American buffalo-hunter must have felt as he began to realize that he had slaughtered all the game. Sometimes a month or more would pass without our ever sighting a possible prize and we were forced to take a decision: either we must risk the wrath of the two main Powers and begin to attack their shipping, or we must go for smaller game. Both prospects were unpleasant. We should not last long against the Powers and none of us would enjoy the sordid business of taking on craft not of our size. The only alternative would be to join the navy of one of the smaller neutral nations. There was no doubt that we should be welcomed with relief into their service (for we had been a thorn in their side as pirates and they would rather have a ship of our tonnage working with them—most would prefer to forget any thoughts of revenge), but it would not be pleasant to accept their discipline after having had virtually the freedom of the high seas. For all that I had reservations, mine was the chief voice raised in support of this latter scheme, and slowly I won Korzeniowski over to the idea. He was an intelligent, far-sighted skipper, and could see that his days as a pirate were numbered. He confided to me that he had yet another consideration.

"I could always scupper the *Lola Montez* and retire," he told me. "I'd be welcome enough in the Islands. But I'm afraid of the boredom. I once entertained the notion of writing novels, you know. I always felt I had a book or two in me. But the notion isn't as attractive as it once was—for who would read me? Who, indeed, would publish me? And I can't say I'm optimistic about writing for posterity when posterity might not even exist! No, I think you're right, Bastable. Time for a new adventure. There are still a couple of largish navies in South America and Indo-China. There are even one or two in Africa. I had hoped that one of the Scandinavian countries would employ us, but yesterday's news has scotched that scheme."

The previous day we had heard that the armies of the Black Attila had finally reached Northern Europe and overrun the last bastions of Western culture. The stories of what had been done to the Swedes, the Danes and the Norwegians chilled my blood. Now black chieftains rode through the streets of Stockholm in the carriages of the murdered Royal Family and the citizens of Oslo had been enslaved, piecemeal, to build the vast generators and chemical plants required to power the mobile war machines of the Black Horde. There had been no-one to enslave in Copenhagen, for the city had resisted a massive siege and now nothing remained of it but smoking rubble.

Brooding on this, Korzeniowski added a little later: "The other argument against retiring to the Islands is, of course, the rumour that the Black Attila has plans to invade Britain. If he did so, sooner or later the Highlands and Islands would be threatened."

"I can't bear to think of that," I said. "But if it did happen, I would be for carrying on some sort of guerrilla war against him. We'd go under, sooner or later, but we'd have done something..."

Korzeniowski smiled. "I have no special loyalties to Britain, Bastable. What makes you think I'd agree to such a scheme?"

I was nonplused. Then his smile broadened. "But I would, of course. The Scots have been good to me. If I have any sort of homeland now I suppose it is in the Outer Hebrides. However, I have a hunch that the black conquest of Britain would only be a token affair. Cicero Hood has his eye on larger spoils."

General Cicero Hood (or so he called himself) was the military genius now known as the Black Attila. We had heard that he was not a native of Africa, at all, but had been born in Arkansas, the son of a slave. It was logical to suspect that his next main objective would be the United States of America (though "United" meant precious little these days), if his main motive for attacking the Western nations was revenge upon the White Race for the supposed ills it had done him and his people.

I commented on the massive egotism of the man. Even his namesake had somewhat nobler motives than simple vengeance in releasing his Huns upon the world.

"Certainly," agreed Korzeniowski, "but there is a messianic quality about Hood. He pursues the equivalent of a religious *jehad* against the enslavers of his people. We have had leaders like that in Poland. You would not understand such feelings, I suppose, being British, but I think I can. Moreover, whatever your opinion of his character (and we know little of that, really), you must admit that he is something of a genius. First he united a vast number of disparate tribes and countries, fired them with his ideals, and worked with amazing speed and skill to make those ideals reality."

I said that I did not doubt his ability as a strategist or, indeed, his intelligence, but it seemed to me that he had perverted a great gift to a mean-spirited ambition.

Korzeniowski only added: "But then, Mr. Bastable, you are not a Negro."

I hardly saw the point of this remark, but dropped the subject, since there was nothing more I had to say on it.

It was perhaps ironic, therefore, that a couple of months later, having sounded out possible 'employers', we sailed for Bantustan with the intention of joining that country's navy.

Bantustan had been better known in my own world as South Africa. It had been one of the first colonies to make a bid for independence during those pre-war years when O'Bean's inventions had released the world from poverty and ignorance. Under the leadership of a young politician of Indian parentage

called Gandhi, it had succeeded in negotiating a peaceful
withdrawal from the British Empire, almost without the Empire
realizing what had happened. Naturally, the great wealth of
Bantustan—its diamonds and its gold alone—was not something
which British, Dutch and American interests had wished to give
up easily, yet Gandhi had managed to placate them by offering
them large shareholdings in the mines without their having to
invest any further capital. Since most of the companies had been
public ones, shareholders' meetings had all voted for Gandhi's
schemes. Then the war had come and there was no longer any
need to pay dividends to the dead and the lost. Bantustan had
prospered greatly during and after the war and was well on its
way to becoming an important and powerful force in the post-
war political game. By building up its military strength, by
signing pacts with General Hood which ensured him of important
supplies of food and minerals at bargain prices, President Gandhi
had protected his neutrality. Bantustan was probably one of the
safest and most stable small nations in the world, and since it
required our experience and our ship, it was the obvious choice
for us. Moreover, we were assured, we should find no racialistic
nonsense there. Black, brown and white races lived together in
harmony—a model to the rest of the world. My only reservations
concerned the political system operating there. It was a republic
based upon the theories of a German dreamer and arch-socialist
called Karl Marx. This man, who in fact lived a large part of his
life in a tolerant England, had made most radicals sound like the
highest of High Tories, and personally I regarded his ideas as at
best unrealistic and at worst morally and socially dangerous. I
doubted if his main theories could have worked in any society
and I expected to have quick proof of this as soon as we docked
in Cape Town.

* * *

We arrived in Cape Town on 14th September, 1906, and were impressed not only by a serviceable fleet of surface and underwater ships, but also a large collection of shipyards working at full capacity. For the first time I was able to see what O'Bean's world must have been like before the war. A great, clean city of tall, beautiful buildings, its streets filled with gliding electric carriages, criss-crossed by public monorail lines, the skies above it full of individual airboats and large, stately airships, both commercial and military. Well-fed, well-dressed people of all colours strolled through wide, tree-lined arcades, and the London I had visited in some other 1973 seemed as far behind this Cape Town as my own London had seemed behind that London of the future.

Suddenly it did not seem to matter what political theories guided the ruling of Bantustan, for it was obvious that it scarcely mattered, so rich was the country and so contented were its people. We had no difficulty in communicating with our new colleagues, for although the official language was Bantu, everyone spoke English and many also spoke Afrikaans, which is essentially Dutch. Here there had been no South African war and as a result there had been little bitterness between the English and Dutch settlers, who had formed a peaceful alliance well before President Gandhi had risen to political power. Seeing what South Africa had become, I almost wept for the rest of the world. If only it had followed this example! I felt prepared to spend my life in the service of this country and give it my loyalty as I had once given Britain my loyalty.

President Gandhi personally welcomed us. He was a small gnome-like man, still quite young, with an infectious smile. In recent years he had devoted quite a lot of his energies to attracting what remained of the West's skilled and talented people to Bantustan. He dreamed of a sane and tranquil world in which all that was best in mankind might flourish. It was his regret that he needed to maintain a strong military position (and thus in his opinion waste resources) in order to guard against attack from outside, but he managed it gracefully enough and felt, he told us at the private dinner to which Korzeniowski and myself were invited, that there was some chance of setting an example to men like Cicero Hood.

"Perhaps he will begin to see how wasteful his schemes are, how his talents could be better put to improving the world and making it into a place where all races live in equality and peace together."

I am not sure that, presented with these ideas in my own world, I could have agreed wholeheartedly with President Gandhi, but the proof of what he said lay all around us. O'Bean had thought that material prosperity was enough to abolish strife and fear, but Gandhi had shown that a clear understanding of the subtler needs of mankind was also necessary—that a moral example had to be made, that a moral life had to be led without compromise—that hypocrisy (albeit unconscious) among a nation's leaders led to cynicism and violence among the population. Without guile, without deceiving those he represented, President Gandhi had laid the foundations for lasting happiness in Bantustan.

"This is, indeed, a haven of civilization you have here," Captain Korzeniowski said approvingly, as we sat on a wide verandah overlooking the great city of Cape Town and smoked excellent local cigars, drinking a perfect home-produced port. "But you are so rich, President Gandhi. Can you protect your country from those who would possess your wealth?"

And then the little Indian gave Korzeniowski and myself a shy, almost embarrassed look. He fingered his tie and stared at the roof-tops of the nearby buildings, and he sounded a trifle sad. "It is something I wished to speak of later," he said. "You are aware, I suppose, that Bantustan has never spilled blood on behalf of its ideals."

"Indeed we are!" I said emphatically.

"It never shall," he said. "In no circumstances would I be responsible for the taking of a single life."

"Only if you were attacked," I said. "Then you would have to defend your country. That would be different."

But President Gandhi shook his head. "You have just taken service in a navy, gentlemen, which exists for only one reason. It is effective only while it succeeds in dissuading those we fear from invading us. It is an expensive and impressive scarecrow. But it is, while I command it, as capable of doing harm as any scarecrow you will find erected by a farmer to frighten the birds away from his fields. If we are ever invaded, it will be your job to take as many people aboard as possible and evacuate them to some place of relative safety. This is a secret that we share. You must guard it well. All our officers have been entrusted with the same secret."

The enormity of President Gandhi's risk in revealing this plan took my breath away. I said nothing.

Korzeniowski frowned and considered this news carefully before replying. "You place a heavy burden on our shoulders, President."

"I wish that I did not have to, Captain Korzeniowski."

"It would only take one traitor…" He did not finish his sentence.

Gandhi nodded. "Only one and we should be attacked and overwhelmed in a few hours. But I rely on something else, Captain Korzeniowski. People like General Hood cannot believe in pacifism. If a traitor did go to him and inform him of the truth, there is every chance that he would not believe it." He grinned like a happy child. "You know of the Japanese method of fighting called Jiu-Jit-Su? You use your opponent's own violence against him. Hopefully, that is what I do with General Hood. Violent men believe only in such concepts as 'weakness' and 'cowardice'. They are so deeply cynical, so rooted in their own insane beliefs, that they cannot even begin to grasp the concept of 'pacifism'. Suppose you were a spy sent by General Hood to find out my plans. Suppose you left here now and went back to the Black Attila and said to him, 'General, President Gandhi has a large, well-equipped army, an air fleet and a navy, but he does not intend to use them if you attack him.' What would General Hood do? He would almost certainly laugh at you, and when you insisted that this was a fact he would probably have you locked up or executed as a fool who had ceased to be of use to him." President Gandhi grinned again. "There is less danger, gentlemen, in living according to a set of high moral principles than most politicians believe."

And now our audience was over. President Gandhi wished us happiness in our new life and we left his quarters in a state of considerable confusion.

It was only when we got to our own ship and crossed the gangplank to go aboard, seeing the hundred or so similar craft all about us, that Korzeniowski snorted with laughter and shook his head slowly from side to side.

"Well, Bastable, what does it feel like to be part of the most expensive scarecrow the world has ever known?"

CHAPTER SEVEN

A Legend in the Flesh

A peaceful year passed in Bantustan—peaceful for us, that is. Reports continued to reach us of the ever-increasing conquests of the Black Attila. We learned that he had raised his flag over the ruins of London and left a token force there, but had met with no real resistance and seemed, as we had guessed, content (like the Romans before him) to claim the British Isles as part of his new Empire without, at this moment in time, making any particular claims upon the country.

Our friends in the Outer Hebrides would be safe for at least a while longer. Our most strenuous duties were to take part in occasional naval manoeuvres, or to escort cargo ships along the coasts of Africa. These ships were crewed entirely by Negroes and we rarely had sight of land. It was regarded as politic for whites not to reveal themselves, even though Hood knew they were not discriminated against in Bantustan.

We had a great deal of leisure and spent it exploring President Gandhi's magnificent country. Great game reserves had been made of the wild veldt and jungle and silent airboats carried one over them so that one could observe all kinds of wildlife in its natural state without disturbing it. There was no hunting here, and lions, elephants, zebra, antelope, wildebeest, rhinoceri, roamed the land unharmed by Man. I could not help, sometimes, making a comparison with the Garden of Eden, where Man and Beast had lived side by side in harmony. Elsewhere we found model farms and mines, worked entirely by automatic machinery, continuing to add to the wealth of the country and, ultimately, the dignity of its inhabitants. Processing plants—for food as well as minerals—lay close to the coast where the food in particular was being stockpiled. Bantustan had more than enough to serve her own needs and the surplus was being built up or sold at cost to the poorer nations. I had begun to wonder why so much food was being stored in warehouses when President Gandhi called a meeting of a number of his air- and sea-officers and told us of a plan he had had for some time.

"All over the world there are people reduced to the level of savage beasts," he said. "They are brutes, but it is no fault of their own. They are brutes because they are hungry and because they live in fear. Therefore, over the last few years I have been putting aside a certain percentage of our food and also medical supplies—serums which my chemists have developed to cope with the various plagues still lingering in Europe and parts of Asia. You all know the function of your fleets is chiefly to give Bantustan security, but it has seemed a shame to waste so much potential, and now I will tell you of my dream."

He paused, giving us all that rather shy, winning smile for which he was famous. "You do not have to share it. I am asking only for volunteers, for there is danger involved. I want to distribute that food and medicine where it is most needed. You, Mr. Bastable, have seen and reported what has happened in Southern England. Would you not agree that these supplies would help to alleviate some of the worst aspects of the conditions there?"

I nodded. "I think so, sir."

"And you, Mr. Caponi," said the President, addressing the dashing and idealistic young Sicilian aviator who had made such a name for himself when he had almost single-handedly saved the survivors of Chicago from the raging fires which had swept that city, by dropping again and again into the inferno, risking almost certain death to rescue the few who remained alive. "You have told me how your countrymen have turned to cannibalism and reverted to their old, feuding ways. You would see that changed, would you not?"

Caponi nodded eagerly, his eyes blazing. "Give me the supplies, Mr. President, and I will have my keels over Sicily by morning!"

Most of the other commanders echoed Captain Caponi's sentiments and President Gandhi was well pleased by their response.

"There are matters I must attend to before we embark on this scheme," he said, "but we can probably begin loading the food and medicine by the end of the month. In the meantime I had better warn you, gentlemen, that General Hood is soon to make a state visit to Bantustan."

The news was received with consternation by most of us—and with undisguised disgust by some, including Caponi, who was never one to hide his feelings. He expressed what a good many of us—particularly the whites—refrained from saying:

"The man is a mass-murderer! A bloody-handed looter! A maniac! Many of us have had relatives done to death by his minions! Why, I have sworn that if I should ever have the opportunity, I should kill him—with my bare hands I should kill him!"

The little President glanced at the floor in some embarrassment. "I hope you will not be so tempted, Captain Caponi, when General Hood is here as my guest…"

"Your guest!" Caponi clapped his hand to his forehead. "Your *guest*!" He broke into a stream of Sicilian oaths which I, for one, was glad I did not understand—although the import of the language was clear enough.

President Gandhi let him continue for a while and then interrupted mildly: "Would it not be better, *capitano*, to have this man as our guest—rather than as our conqueror? By meeting him, I hope to influence him—to beg him to stop the senseless warfare, this vendetta against the white race which can only lead to more violence, more terror, more grief…"

Caponi spread his hands, his somewhat pudgy features displaying an expression which was almost pitying. "You think he will listen, Mr. President? Such a man cannot be reasoned with! I know to my sorrow how destructive a vendetta can be—but the Black Attila is a madman—a wild beast—a ferocious and senseless killer—a torturer of women and children. Oh, sir, you are too unworldly…"

President Gandhi raised his eyebrows, biting his lip. He sighed. "I hope I am not," he said. "I understand all the arguments and I know how you must feel. But I must obey my conscience. I must make an effort to reason with General Hood."

Captain Caponi turned away. "Very well—reason with him—and see what good it does. Can you reason with a whirlwind? Can you reason with a rogue rhino? Reason with him, President Gandhi—and pray for the safety of your country!" And with that he walked rapidly from the room.

One or two of the other officers mumbled words which echoed Caponi's. We all loved President Gandhi, but we all felt that he was misguided in his hopes.

Finally, he said: "Well, gentlemen, I hope some of you will agree to be present at the banquet I intend to hold for General Hood. If your voices are added to mine, at least you will know, as I will know, that you have done your best…"

He dismissed us, then, and we all left with heavy hearts, speculating variously on what General Hood would be like to meet in the flesh and how we should react when—or if—we saw him.

Personally I had mixed feelings. It was not every day, after all, that one received the opportunity of dining with a legend, a world-conquering tyrant whom history would rank with Genghis Khan or Alexander the Great. I was determined to accept the President's invitation. Besides, I had to admit that I was beginning to get a little bored with my life in Bantustan. I was first and foremost a soldier, a man of action, trained in a certain way of life and not, by nature, contemplative or much of an intellectual. General Hood's visit would, if nothing else, relieve that boredom for a while!

A week later there was a Black Fleet hanging in the skies of Cape Town. Between twenty and thirty good-sized keels lay anchored to specially built masts. They swayed slightly in the warm wind from the west, each of them displaying the insignia of the Black Attila's so-called New Ashanti Empire: a black, rampant, snarling African lion in a scarlet circle. Hood *claimed* as an ancestor the famous Quacoo Duah, King of Ashanti in the 1860s, and it was initially on the Gold Coast that he had begun to build his army—starting with a handful of Ashanti and Fanti nationalists pledged to the overthrow of the first native government of Ashantiland (as it had been renamed after Independence). Although the Black Horde consisted of members of all African peoples, as well as those from beyond Africa, it had somehow retained the name of Ashanti, just as the Roman Empire had kept its name even after it had few connections with Rome at all. Also the Ashanti people were well-respected throughout most of Africa, and since Hood claimed to be Quacoo Duah's direct descendant, it suited him to keep the name.

Many of those who had sworn to have nothing whatsoever to do with the whole affair were drawn reluctantly to the streets or their balconies, to watch the descent of Cicero Hood and his retinue from the flagship (diplomatically named the *Chaka*) which hung just above the main formation. For the first time we saw Hood's famous Lion Guard—huge, perfectly formed warriors with skin like polished ebony and proud, handsome features, drawn from all the tribes of Africa. On their heads were steel caps from which projected tall, nodding ostrich plumes dyed scarlet and orange. From their shoulders hung short cloaks made from the manes and skins of male lions. They wore short, sleeveless jackets of midnight blue, similar to the jackets worn by French Zouaves, trimmed with gold and silver braid, and tight cavalry-style britches to match. High boots of black, gleaming leather were on their feet and each man carried two weapons, symbolic of the Old and the New Africa—an up-to-date carbine on the back and a long-shafted, broad-bladed spear in the right hand. Standing in the open-air carriages, scarcely moving a muscle, their faces expressionless, they were undoubtedly amongst the most impressive soldiers in the world. Their carriages formed a perfect circle around that of General Cicero Hood himself—a carriage painted in splendid colours and flying the black-and-scarlet flag of the Black Attila's Empire. From where I stood on the roof of my apartment building (many of my colleagues were with me, including Korzeniowski) I could see that there were two figures in the carriage, but I was too far away to make out details of their features, though it seemed to me that one of the occupants was white!

Upon landing, Hood and his Guard transferred to open electrical broughams and began a long procession through the streets of Cape Town that was received with surprising enthusiasm from many of the citizens (admittedly most of them Negroes), but I could see little of this procession from my vantage-point. I retired to the bar downstairs where a number of other officers were coming back from the street, where they had witnessed the scene. Not a few of the white and a number of the black officers had looks of grudging admiration on their faces, for there had been no doubt about the excellence of the stage-management involved in Hood's arrival. A man I knew slightly who had been a land-fleet commander in India before he had joined the army of Bantustan (his name, as I recall, was Laurence), ordered himself a stiff brandy and drained it in a single swallow before turning to me and saying in a tone of awe: "I say, Bastable, the chap's got a bally white woman in tow. Rum go, eh? His distaste for us doesn't seem to extend to the female of the species, what?"

Another acquaintance called Horton, who had been an officer in the Sierra Leone navy before the nation was annexed by Hood, said dryly: "To the victor the spoils, old man." There was a look of amusement on his brown face, and he winked at me, enjoying Laurence's discomfort.

"Well, I mean to say…" began Laurence, realizing his lack of tact. "It's not that I feel…"

"It's just that you do." Horton laughed and turned to order Laurence another drink. "You think Hood's taken a white concubine as a sort of gesture. It could be that he finds her so attractive he doesn't care what colour she is. I've heard of Europeans falling in love with African women. Haven't you?"

Laurence's next point was undeniably a good one. "But not Europeans with a deep loathing of Negroes, Horton. I mean, it rather shakes his case about us being awful fiends, doesn't it?"

Horton grinned. "Maybe he prefers the devil he knows."

"I must admit," put in a lieutenant who had begun his career in the Russian navy, Nicolai, "I wouldn't mind knowing her myself. What a beauty! I think she's the most ravishing creature I've ever seen. Good luck to Hood on that score, say I!"

The conversation continued on these lines for a while until those of us who had accepted invitations to attend the banquet had to leave to get ready. Korzeniowski and I and a party of other 'underwater sailors' were going together. Dressed in the simple, white dress-uniforms of the Bantustan navy, we left for the palace in a large carriage rather like an electrically powered *char-à-banc*, were met at the steps and escorted into the great hall which normally housed the elected representatives of the people of Bantustan. Long tables had been laid out and each place was adorned with gold and silver plate and cutlery. We were privileged (if that is the word) to sit at the President's table and would thus be afforded a good chance of observing the infamous General Hood at close range.

When we were all seated, President Gandhi, General Hood and the general's lady consort entered through a door in the back of the hall and moved to take their places at the table.

I believe that I had by this time learned enough self-control not to register my surprise upon recognizing the woman whose hand was now placed on the arm of the despot who had become master of most of Africa and all of Europe. Our eyes met and she acknowledged me with a ghost of a smile before turning her head to say something to Hood. It was Una Persson! Now I knew why she had wished to return to Africa so speedily and why she had been reluctant to take me with her. Had she, even then, been keeping this association with the Black Attila?

General Hood was not what I expected. He was as tall as any member of his "Lion Guard", but fairly slender, moving with what I can only describe as a sort of awkward grace. He wore perfectly cut conventional evening-dress which was entirely without decoration. I had expected a fierce-eyed warlord, but this man was close to middle age, with the distinguished air of a high-ranking diplomat. His hair and beard were greying a little and his large, dark eyes held a mildness which could only be deceptive. I was reminded, against my will, of a sort of black Abraham Lincoln!

President Gandhi was beaming. It seemed he had had a conversation with General Hood which had proved satisfactory to him. The little Indian was dressed, as always, in a light cotton suit of what we used to term "Bombay cut". They took their places and we, who had been standing, resumed ours. The meal began in a rather grim silence, but slowly the atmosphere improved. General Hood chatted amiably to President Gandhi, to the President's aides, and to Una Persson. I heard a little of the conversation— enough to know that it was the usual sort of polite small-talk which goes on among politicians on occasions like this one. From what might have been a mistaken sense of tact, I tried not to look at Mrs. Persson during the dinner and addressed myself primarily to the lady on my left who seemed to be obsessed with the notion of trying to breed back, in Africa, many of the species of bird-life which had been made all but extinct during the wars in Europe.

The meal was an excellent compromise between European and African dishes, and I think it is probably the best I have ever eaten, but we were on the sweet course before I was saved from the conversation of the amateur ornithologist on my left. Quite suddenly I heard the deep, mellow tones of General Hood speaking my name and I looked up in some embarrassment.

"You are Mr. Bastable, then?"

I stuttered a reply to the effect that his information was correct. I was not even sure how one addressed a despotic conqueror who had on his hands the blood of hundreds of thousands of innocents.

"You have my gratitude, Mr. Bastable."

I was conscious of a decided lull in the conversation around me and I think I might have been blushing a little. I noticed that Mrs. Persson was smiling broadly at me, as was President Gandhi, and I felt very foolish, for no particular reason.

"I have, sir?" was, I think, what I answered. It sounded insane to my ears and I tried to recover my equilibrium by reminding myself that this man, in spite of appearances, was the sworn enemy of my race. It was, however, difficult to maintain an attitude of disdain while at the same time behaving in a way which suited the social situation. I had accepted the invitation to dine at the palace and therefore had a duty to President Gandhi not to offend his guests.

General Hood laughed a deep, full-throated laugh. "You saved the life of someone I hold very dear." He patted Una Persson's hand. "Surely you remember, Mr. Bastable?"

I said that it had been nothing, that anyone would have done the same, and so on.

"You showed great courage, Mrs. Persson tells me."

I made no answer to this. Then General Hood added: "Indeed, if it had not been for you, Mr. Bastable, it is unlikely that I should have been able to continue with certain military ambitions I have been entertaining. White though your skin is, I think you have the heart of a black man."

A calculated irony, surely! He had managed to implicate me in his crimes and I think relished my embarrassment. Next he added:

"If, at any time, you wish to leave the employment of Bantustan, the Ashanti Empire could make use of your services. After all, you have already proved your loyalty to our cause."

I saw the eyes of all the whites in the hall staring at me. It was too much. Seized by anger, I blurted back: "I regret, sir, that my loyalty is to the cause of peace and the rebuilding of a sane world. The cold-blooded murder of the women and children of my own race is not something to which I could easily lend myself!"

Now the silence in the hall was total, but General Hood soon broke the atmosphere by leaning back in his chair, smiling and shaking his head. "Mr. Bastable, I have no dislike of the white man. In his place, he performs a large number of useful functions.

I employ white men in a good many capacities. Indeed, there are individuals who show all the qualities I would value in an African. Such individuals are given every opportunity to shine in the Ashanti Empire. You have a poor impression of me, I fear—whereas I have nothing but respect for you." He raised his glass to toast me. "Your health, Mr. Bastable. I am sincere in my offer. President Gandhi and I have been discussing exchanging emissaries. I shall put in a strong plea to him that you be among those invited to New Kumasi. There you shall see for yourself if I am the tyrant you have heard about."

I was far too angry by now to make any sort of reply. President Gandhi tactfully drew General Hood into conversation and a little later Korzeniowski came up behind me and tapped me on the shoulder, leading me from the hall.

My emotions were, to put it mildly, mixed. I was torn between boiling anger, social embarrassment, loyalty to President Gandhi and his dream of peace, as well as my own responses to Hood himself. It was no surprise, now, that he had risen so swiftly to eminence in the world. Tyrant and murderer he might be, but it was undeniable that he had a magnetic personality, that he had the power to charm even those who hated him most. I had expected a swaggering barbarian and had encountered, instead, a sophisticated politician, an American (I learned later) who had been educated at Oxford and Heidelberg and whose academic career had been an outstanding one before he put down his books and picked up the sword. I was shaking and close to tears as Korzeniowski took me back to my quarters and devoted himself to calming me down. But it was hours before I finished my mindless ranting. I drank a good deal, too, and I think that it was a combination of alcohol and emotional exhaustion which finally shut me up. One moment I was raging at the insults of the Black Attila and the next moment I had fallen face-forward to the floor.

Korzeniowski must have put me to bed. In the morning

I woke up with the worst headache of my life, still in a filthy temper, but no longer capable of expressing it. It was a knocking at the door which had awakened me. My batman answered it and a short while later brought me my breakfast tray. On the tray was an envelope bearing the seal of the President himself. I pushed the tray aside and inspected the envelope, hardly daring to open it. Doubtless it contained some kind of reproof for my behaviour of the previous evening, but I was unrepentant.

I lay in bed, the envelope still in my hand, considering the answers I should have given Hood if I had had my wits about me.

I was determined not to be charmed by him, to judge him only by his actions, to remember how whole European cities had been destroyed by him and their populations enslaved. I regretted that I had mentioned none of this during our encounter. I have never believed in violent solutions to political problems, but I felt if there was one man who deserved to be assassinated it was Cicero Hood. The fact that he had received an excellent education only made him more of a villain in my eyes, for he had perverted that education in order to pursue his racial *jehad*. He might blandly deny his policies of genocide, but what he had done in the past few years spoke for itself. At that moment, I felt I could, like Caponi, cheerfully kill him with my bare hands.

It was Korzeniowski turning up that forced me to control myself. He stood at the end of my bed, looking down at me with a kind of sympathetic irony, asking me how I felt.

"Not too good," I told him. I showed him the letter. "I think I'm due for the sack. I'll be leaving Bantustan soon enough, I shouldn't wonder."

"But you haven't opened the letter, old man."

I handed it up to him. "You open it. Tell me the worst."

Korzeniowski went to my desk and took a paper-knife to slit the top of the envelope. He removed the contents—a single sheet of paper—and read it out in his precise, guttural English:

"Dear Mr. Bastable. If you have the time today, I should be grateful if you would visit me in my office. About five would be convenient for me, if that would suit you.

Yours sincerely, Gandhi."

Korzeniowski handed me the letter. "Typical of him," he said admiringly. "If you have time, Mr. Bastable. He is giving you the option. I shouldn't have thought that meant a carpeting, old chap, would you?"

I read the letter for myself, frowning. "Then what on earth does it mean?" I said.

CHAPTER EIGHT
A Decision in Cold Blood

Needless to say, although I hemmed and hawed a lot, I eventually arrived, scrubbed and neat, at the presidential palace at five o'clock sharp and was immediately escorted into President Gandhi's office. The office was as plain and functional as all the rooms he used. He sat behind his desk looking, for him, decidedly stern, and I guessed that, after all, I was in for a wigging, that my resignation would be demanded. So I stood smartly to attention and prepared myself to take whatever the President was about to give me.

He got up, rubbing his balding head with the palm of his hand, his spectacles gleaming in the sun which flooded through the open window. "Please sit down, captain." It was rare for him to use a military title. I did as I was ordered.

"I have had a long talk with General Hood today," Gandhi began. "We have, as you know, been discussing ways of cementing good relations between Bantustan and the New Ashanti Empire. On most matters we have reached an amicable understanding, but there is one detail which concerns you. You know that I believe in free will, that it is not part of my beliefs to force a man to do something he does not wish to do. So I will put the situation to you and you must make up your own mind about it. General Hood was not joking last night when he offered you employment…"

"Not joking? I hoped so, sir. I do not wish to be employed as a mass-murderer…"

President Gandhi raised his hand. "Of course not. But General Hood, it seems, has taken a liking to you. He admired the way in which you answered him back last night."

"I thought it a poor performance. I meant to apologize, sir."

"No, no. I understand your position completely. You showed great self-control. Perhaps that was what Hood was doing—testing you. He is genuinely grateful for the part you played, apparently, in saving Mrs. Persson's life in England—and, I could be completely wrong, but I have the feeling he wants to vindicate himself in your eyes. Perhaps he sees you as representative of—in his terms—the better sort of white man. Perhaps he is tired of killing and actually does want to begin building a safer and saner world—though his present military plans seem to contradict that. Whatever the reason, Bastable, he has insisted that you be part of the diplomatic mission sent to his capital at New Kumasi—indeed, he has made it a condition. You will be the only, um, white member of the mission. Unless you go, he refuses to continue with our negotiations."

"Well, sir, if those are not the actions of a madman, a despot, I do not know what they are!" I replied.

"Certainly, they are not based on the kind of logic I recognize. General Hood is used to having his way—particularly when it comes to the fate of white men. I do not deny that. However, you know how important these talks are to me. I hope to influence the general—at least to temper his future policies towards those he conquers. Everything I have dreamed of is endangered—unless you consider that you can accept his terms. You must look to your own conscience, Mr. Bastable. I do not want to influence you, I have already gone against my principles—I am aware that I am putting moral pressure on you. You must forget what I want and do only what you think is right."

It was then that I reached what was perhaps the most cold-blooded decision of my life. If I accepted, then I should be in an excellent position to get close to Hood and, if necessary, put an end to his ambitions for good and all. I had contemplated assassination—now I was being given the opportunity to perform it. I decided that I *would* go to New Kumasi. I *would* observe the Black Attila's actions for myself. I would be Hood's jury and his judge. And if I decided that he was guilty—then I would take it upon myself to be his executioner!

Naturally, I said nothing of this to President Gandhi. Instead, I frowned, pretending to consider what he had said to me.

I think I was a little mad, then. It seems so to me now. The strain of finding myself in yet another version of history, of being in no way in control of my own destiny, was probably what influenced me to seek to alter events in this world. Still, I will not try to justify myself. The fact remains that I had decided to become, if necessary, a murderer! I will leave it to you, the reader, to decide on what sort of morality it is that justifies such a decision.

At last I looked up at President Gandhi and said:

"When would I have to leave, sir?"

Gandhi seemed relieved. "Within two weeks. I must select the other members of the mission."

"Have you any idea, sir, what part Mrs. Persson has played in this?"

"No," he admitted. "No clear idea. It could be quite a large one, for all I know. She seems to have considerable influence with General Hood. She is an extremely enigmatic woman."

I was bound to agree with him.

* * *

t was with great regret that I said goodbye to Captain Korzeniowski and the other friends I had made in Cape Town. All felt that I had been forced into this position and I wished that I might confide in them my secret decision, but of course it was impossible. To share a secret is to share a burden and I had no intention of placing any part of such a burden on the shoulders of anyone else.

President Gandhi was sending some of his best people to New Kumasi—ten men, three women and myself. The others were either of Asian or African origin or of mixed blood. As the only white I did not feel out of place in their company, for I had long since become used to the easy terms on which the races mingled in Bantustan. In his choice, President Gandhi had shown that he was a shrewd as well as an idealistic politician, for two of the members of the mission were military experts briefed to observe all they could of General Hood's war-making capacity and discover as much intelligence as possible in respect of his long-term military ambitions. All, with the possible exception of myself, believed heart and soul in Gandhi's ideals.

The day came when we were ferried up to the waiting aerial frigate. Its hull was a gleaming white and it hung in the deep, blue sky like some perfectly symmetrical cloud, with the plain, pale-green flag of Bantustan flying from its rigging.

Within moments of our going aboard, the ship dropped its anchor-cables and began to head north-west towards the shining waters of St. Helena Bay.

I looked back at the slender spires of Cape Town and wondered if I should ever see that city of my friends again. Then I put such thoughts from my head and gave myself up to polite conversation with my colleagues, all of whom were speculating on what they would find in New Kumasi and how we might expect to be treated if relations between New Ashanti and Bantustan became strained. None of us was used to dealing with despots who had absolute powers of life and death over their subjects.

Twenty-four hours passed as we crossed the greater part of western Africa and hung, at last, in the air over General Cicero Hood's capital.

It was very different from Cape Town. Those new buildings which had been erected were of a distinctly African character and not, I must admit, unpleasant to look upon. A preponderance of cylindrical shapes topped by conical roofs reminded one somewhat of the kind of huts found in a typical kraal in the old days—but these "huts" were many storeys high and built of steel, glass, concrete and modern alloys. The city was unusual, too, in that it seemed to be walled in the medieval manner, and on the walls was evidence that New Kumasi had been designed as a fortress—large guns could be seen, as well as 'pillbox' emplacements. The grandiose, barbaric lion flag of the Ashanti Empire flew everywhere, and military airships cruised around the perimeters like guardian birds of prey. Here there were no monorails or moving pavements or any of the other public-transport amenities of Bantustan's cities, but it was a well-run metropolis, as far as one could see—very much under the control of the army. Indeed, half the people I saw, after we had landed, were in uniform—both men and women. There was no sign of poverty, but no sign, either, of the bountiful wealth of Cape Town. The majority of the population were Negro and the only whites I saw seemed to be doing fairly menial tasks (one or two of the porters at the aerodrome were European) but were not evidently ill-treated. There were very few private vehicles in the streets, but a good many public omnibuses of, for this world, a slightly old-fashioned sort, running off wire-borne electrical current. Other than these, there were chiefly military vehicles moving about. Huge land ironclads rolled up and down the thoroughfares, evidently taking precedence over other vehicles.

These were of the globular pattern, mounted on a wheeled frame but able, at a pinch, to release themselves from the frame and roll under their own volition, their speed and course being checked by telescopic legs which could be extended from most points on the hull. I had heard of these machines, but had never seen one at close quarters. If released upon a town, or an enemy position, they were capable of flattening it in moments without firing a shot from their steam-powered gatlings and electrical cannon. I could imagine the terror one might feel when such a monster came rolling towards one!

In contrast, the Guard of Honour which greeted us and escorted us to General Hood's headquarters was mounted on tall, white stallions, and the carriages into which we climbed were much more familiar to me than the rest of my colleagues—for they were horse-drawn, rather like the landaus of my own world. The nodding plumes of the Lion Guard horsemen flanking us, the discipline with which they sat their mounts, reminded me graphically of that world which I so longed to return to but which, now, I was reconciled never to seeing again.

The Imperial Palace of New Ashanti recalled, in its impressive beauty, what I had seen of the famous Benin culture. Like so many of the other buildings, it was cylindrical and topped by a conical roof which stretched beyond the walls, umbrella-fashion, and was supported by carved pillars, forming a kind of cloister or arcade faced with ivory, gold, bronze and silver, affording shade for the many guards who surrounded it. Every modern material and architectural skill had been used in the building of the palace, yet it was undeniably African, showing hardly any evidence of European influence. I was to learn later that it had been Cicero Hood's firm policy to encourage what he called "the practical arts" in his Empire, and to insist that their expression be distinctly African in conception. As one who had seen many foreign cities of Asia ruined by ugly European-style architecture, who regretted the passing of ethnic and traditional designs in buildings, as well as many other things, I welcomed this aspect of Hood's rule, if no other.

Having had some experience of the petty tyrants of India, I fully expected the Black Attila to behave as they behaved and to keep us waiting for hours in his anterooms before we were granted an audience, but we were escorted rapidly through the exquisitely decorated passages of the palace and into a wide, airy hall lit from above by large windows, its walls covered with friezes and bas-reliefs of traditional African design but showing the events of the recent past in terms of the heroic struggles and triumphs of the New Ashanti Empire. Hood himself was recognizable as featuring in several scenes, including the Conquest of Scandinavia, and there were representations of land fleets, aerial battles, underwater skirmishes and the like, giving the panels a very strange appearance—a mingling of ancient and almost barbaric emotions with examples of the most modern technical achievements of mankind.

At the opposite end of the hall from the great double doors through which we entered stood a dais carpeted in zebra skin, and upon the dais (I was reminded, for a moment, of the King of East Grinstead) was placed a throne of carved ebony, its scarlet, quilted back bearing the lion motif one saw everywhere in New Kumasi.

Dressed in a casual, white tropical suit, Cicero Hood stood near his throne, looking out of a tall window. He turned when we were announced, dismissing the guards with one hand while keeping the other in his trouser pocket, crossing with a light step to a table where there had been arranged a variety of drinks and non-alcoholic beverages (Hood had doubtless been informed that there were several in our party who did not drink). He served each of us personally and then moved about the hall arranging chairs so that we might all be seated close together. No European king could have behaved with greater courtesy to guests he was determined to honour (and yet equally determined to impress, for he had made sure we saw all the outward signs of his power!).

He had taken the trouble to find out the names of each individual in our party and to know something of their interests and special responsibilities in Bantustan and he chatted easily with them, showing a good knowledge of most subjects and ready to admit ignorance where he had it. Again, I was surprised. These were by no means the swaggering ill-manners of a parvenu monarch. There had been kings and emperors in my own world who might have learned much of the art of *noblesse oblige* from the Black Attila.

He did not address me individually until he had talked for a while with the others, then he grinned at me and shook me warmly by the hand and I had the unmistakable impression that the tyrant actually *liked* me—a feeling I could not reciprocate and could not equate with my knowledge of his much-publicized hatred of the white race. My own response was polite, self-controlled, but reserved.

"I am so glad, Mr. Bastable, that you could agree to come," he said.

"I was not aware, sir, that I had a great deal of choice," I answered. "President Gandhi seemed to be under the impression that you had insisted on my being part of the mission."

"I expressed the hope that you might be able to join it, certainly. After all, I must show impartiality." This was said with a smile which doubtless he hoped would disarm me. "The token European, you know."

Deliberately or not, he had made me feel self-conscious by referring to the colour of my skin. Even a joke had the effect of emphasizing the difference we both felt, and it would not have mattered if the man who made it had been my best friend, I should still have had the same feelings, particularly since there were no other whites in the room.

Noting my discomfort, Cicero Hood patted me on the shoulder. "I'm sorry, Mr. Bastable. A remark in bad taste. But hard for the son of a slave to resist, I'm sure you'd agree."

"It would seem to me, sir, that your own success would be sufficient to help you forget any stigma…"

"Stigma, Mr. Bastable?" His voice hardened. "I assure you that I do not feel it is a stigma. The stigma, surely, belongs to those who enslaved my people in the first place."

It was a good point. "Perhaps you are right, sir," I mumbled. I was no match for Hood's intellectual swiftness.

Hood's manner instantly became condescending again. "But you are right. I have mellowed in the last year or two, thanks, in some measure, to the good fortune I have had. I have only one goal left and then I shall be content. However, that goal is the most difficult I have set myself, and I have a feeling I shall meet strong resistance from a certain Power which has, up to now, remained neutral."

"You mean the Australasian-Japanese Federation, sir?" This was Field Marshal Akari, the man we had elected as chief spokesman for our mission. A distinguished officer and one of President Gandhi's oldest friends and supporters, he was owed much by Bantustan and had frequently acted as the President's deputy in the past. "Surely they would not risk everything they have built up over the last few years? They cannot feel threatened by Ashanti!"

"I am afraid that they do, field marshal," said Hood in a tone of the utmost regret. "It would seem that they regard the Pacific as their territory and they have had some news of my plans—I have made no secret of them—and feel that if my ships begin to sail 'their' ocean it will only be a matter of time before I cast greedy eyes upon their islands."

Mrs. Nzinga, but lately Minister of Communications in Gandhi's government, said quietly: "Then you intend to attack the United States? Is that what you mean, sir?"

Hood shrugged. "Attack is not the word I would choose, Mrs. Nzinga. My intention is to liberate the black peoples of the United States, to help them build a new and lasting civilization there. I know that I am thought of as a senseless tyrant by many—embarked upon a crazy course of genocide—a war of attrition against the whites—but I think there is a method to my 'madness'. For too long the so-called 'coloured' peoples of the world have been made to feel inferior by the Europeans. In many parts of Africa an awful, soul-destroying apathy existed until I began to show those I led that the whites had no special skills, no special intelligence, no special rights to rule. My speeches against the whites were calculated, just as my nationalism was calculated. I knew that there was little time, after the war, to make the gains I had to make. I had to use crude methods to build up my resources, my territory, the confidence of those I led. I happen to believe, rightly or wrongly, that it is time the black man had a chance to run the world. I think if he can rid himself of the sickness of European logic, he can make a lasting Utopia. I admire President Gandhi, Mrs. Nzinga—though you might find that strange in a 'bloody-handed tyrant'. I have not threatened Bantustan because I fear your military strength. I want Bantustan to continue to exist because it is a symbol to the rest of the world of an ideal state. But it is Bantustan's *good fortune*, not any special virtue, which has made it what it is. The rest of the world is not so fortunate and if President Gandhi tried to set up his state, say, in India he would find that it would not last for long! First the world must be united—and the way to unite it is to form large empires—and the way to form large empires, I regret, madam, is by war and bloodshed—by ferocious conquest."

"But violence will be met by violence," said Professor Hira, whose university programme had been such a success in Bantustan. A small, tubby man, his shiny face positively glowed with emotion. "Those you conquer will, sooner or later, try to rise up against you. It is in the nature of things."

"Risings of the sort you describe, professor," said General Hood grimly, "are only successful where the government is weak. Tyrannies can last for centuries—have lasted for centuries—if the administration remains firmly in control. If it cultivates in itself the Stoic virtues. If it is, in its own terms, just.

"My Empire has been compared with that of Rome. The Roman Empire did not fall—it withered away when it was no longer of any use. It left behind it a heritage of philosophy alone which has continued to influence us all."

"But you see Western thinking as having brought us to the brink of world annihilation," I put in.

"In some ways only. That is not the point, however. I described an example. I believe that African thinking will produce a saner, more lasting civilization than that of the West."

"You have no proof of this," I said.

"No. But a theory must be tested to be *dis*proved, Mr. Bastable. I intend to test the theory and to ensure that the test is thorough. The experiment will continue long after my death."

There was nothing much I could reply to this without getting involved in abstractions. I subsided.

"You may see my ambitions in America as being motivated merely by revenge," Cicero Hood continued, "but I wish to build something in the country of my birth as strong as that which I am building here. The whites of the United States are decadent—perhaps they have always been decadent. A new enthusiasm, however, can be generated amongst the blacks. I intend to put power into their hands. I intend to liberate America. Have you not heard what is happening there now? Having no real enemy to fight any longer, the whites turn, as always, upon the minorities. They wiped out the Red Indians—now they plan to wipe out the Negroes. It is the spirit of Salem—the corrupting influence of Puritanism which in itself is a perversion of the Stoic ideal—infecting what remains of a nation which could have set an example to the world, just as Bantustan now sets an example. That spirit must be exorcized for good and all. When the whites are conquered they will not be enslaved, as we were enslaved. They will be given a place in the New Ashanti Empire; they will be given a chance to *earn* their way to full equality. I shall take their power from them—but I shall not take their dignity. The two have been confused for too long. But only a black man realizes that—for he has had the *experience* during centuries of exploitation by the whites!"

It was a noble speech (even if I was skeptical of its logic), but I could not resist, at last, making a remark which General Hood was bound to find telling.

"It is possible, General Hood," I said, "that you can convince us that your motives are idealistic, but you have told us yourself that the Australasian-Japanese Federation is not so convinced. There is every chance that they will be able to thwart your scheme. What then? You will have risked everything and achieved nothing. Why not concentrate on building Africa into a single great nation? Forget your hatred of the United States. Let it find its own solutions. The A.J.F. is probably as powerful as the Ashanti Empire..."

"Oh, probably more powerful now!" It was the clear, sweet voice of Una Persson that interrupted me. She had entered through a door behind Hood's throne. "I have just received confirmation, General Hood, of what I suspected. O'Bean is in Tokyo. He has been there, it seems, since the outbreak of the war. He has been convinced that Ashanti represents a further threat to the world.

He has been working on plans for a new fleet for nearly two years. Already a score of his ships have been built in the yards of Sydney and Melbourne and are ready to sail. Unless we mobilize immediately, there is every chance that we shall be defeated."

General Hood's response was unexpected. He looked first at me, then at Una Persson, then he threw back his head and he laughed long and heartily.

"Then we mobilize," he said. "Oh, by all means—we mobilize. I am going home, Mrs. Persson. I am going home!"

BOOK TWO

THE BATTLE FOR WASHINGTON

CHAPTER ONE

The Two Fleets Meet

Looking back, I suppose I should count myself fortunate in being, by a strange set of circumstances, witness to Hood's decision to risk everything he had gained by invading America, and to experience the invasion (and its aftermath) itself. Not many young officers are given such an opportunity.

My determination to take the law into my own hands if I judged Hood "guilty" remained as strong, but I was already beginning to realize that the Black Attila was a far subtler individual than I had at first supposed. Moreover, I soon came to learn that his ferocity, his reputation for putting to death or enslaving whole cities, was something of a myth which he encouraged. It was useful to him if his enemies believed the myth, for it quite often resulted in all but bloodless conquests! The defenders would prefer to parley rather than fight, and would often ask for terms quite inferior to those Hood was prepared to grant! This meant that, when he proposed terms which were better than they had expected, he gained the reputation of munificence which was quite undeserved, but encouraged the conquered to work willingly for him—out of a sense of relief as much as any other consideration!

I saw little of Hood or Una Persson in the following week. They were far too involved in their plans for mobilization. We of the diplomatic mission could only gather what information was available and relay it to Bantustan. We were allowed, in the first days, to communicate information of all kinds freely to our own country, but a little later a certain censorship was imposed as General Hood became nervous of news reaching Tokyo. I think he had heard that the A.J.F. fleet was making for the Atlantic. The largest part of the Ashanti fleet had been based in Europe, where it was most useful, and some ships had to be recalled, while others were ordered to assemble in Hamburg, Copenhagen, Gothenburg and other Northern European ports, preparatory to sailing for America.

I gathered that Hood was not merely relying on his vast land, air and sea fleets, but had another counter to play. From something Una Persson had said, I thought her trip to England had played a part in Hood's 'secret weapon' being developed, but I was to learn more of this later.

My next surprise came a day or two before Hood was due to sail. Una Persson visited me at the legation, where I was busy with some sort of meaningless paperwork. She apologized for disturbing me and said that General Hood would like to see me for a few moments during luncheon.

I went unwillingly. Privately I was sure that the powerful Australasian-Japanese Federation would put a stop to his dreams of conquest for ever and that I no longer had a part to play in the history of this world. I was looking forward to returning to Bantustan when the Ashanti Empire collapsed, as it was bound to do.

Hood had almost finished luncheon when I arrived at the palace. He was sitting at the head of a long table surrounded by his chief ministers and generals. There were charts spread among the remains of a simple meal and black faces were bent over them, conversing in low, urgent tones. All looked up as I arrived, and several frowned, making insulting remarks about their meal being spoiled by the sight of a white man. I had become quite used to this sort of thing from Hood's lieutenants (though, to be fair, not all were so ill-mannered) and was able to ignore the comments, saying: "You sent for me, general?"

Hood seemed surprised to see me. He looked vaguely at me for a moment and then snapped his fingers as if remembering why he had sent for me. "Ah, yes, Mr. Bastable. Just to tell you to have a bag packed by tomorrow morning and to present yourself to the captain of the *Dingiswayo*. He is expecting you. I've exchanged communications with President Gandhi and he is agreeable to the scheme. You have been seconded to my staff. You're coming with us to America, Mr. Bastable. Congratulations."

There was nothing I could say. I tried to think of some retort, failed, and saluted. "Very well, sir." Whether there was some deeper motive involved, or whether this was just another example of Hood's quixotic and whimsical behaviour where my fate was concerned I did not know. It seems that by taking my initial decision I was now bound to follow it through all the way.

And that was how I came to be the only white officer to accompany the sea-borne Black Horde when it sailed out over the Atlantic bound for New York with the express intention of destroying for ever the power of the Caucasian race!

My life has been full of ironies since my first, ill-fated expedition to Teku Benga, but I think that that remains the greatest irony of them all.

Hood had thrown virtually everything he had into the invasion fleet. Surface and underwater vessels, airships of every description, came together at last just off the coast of Iceland—a fleet which filled the sky and occupied the ocean for as far as the eye could see. Aboard the ships were stored Hood's vast collection of land ironclads and in the centre of all these there rose a gigantic hull, specially built but utterly mysterious in its purpose, which could not progress under its own power but which had to be towed by thirty other battleships. I guessed that this must surely be Hood's secret weapon, but neither I nor any of the other officers aboard the *Dingiswayo* had any inkling of its nature!

And all the while news was coming through of the Australasian-Japanese fleet converging on our own.

Hood's hope was that we could run ahead of the A.J.F. fleet and get to the coast of North America before it caught up with us, but these new ships of O'Bean's were much faster than ours (their fire-power was a completely unknown factor) and I knew that we had no chance. There was a school of thought which said that we should disperse our own fleet, but Hood was against this, feeling that we had a better chance if we concentrated our forces. Also, as was evident, he was prepared to risk almost everything to protect the vast hull we towed (or, at least, the contents of the hull) and I had the impression that he might consider sacrificing everything else so long as that hull arrived eventually in New York.

There was scarcely a ship in the fleet which would not have dwarfed one of the ironclads of my own day. Equipped with long-snouted naval guns which could put a stream of incredibly powerful shells into the air in the time it took one of my world's ships to fire a single shot, capable of cruising at speeds reaching ninety knots, of manoeuvring with the speed and ease of the lightest cruiser, a couple of them could have given our good old British navy a pretty grim time. Hood had a hundred of these alone in his fleet, as well as over fifty underwater battleships and nearly seventy big aerial men-o'-war (which, in turn, were equipped with light fighting airboats capable of leaving the mother ship, striking rapidly at an enemy and returning to safety above the clouds). As well as this massive fighting strength, there

were dozens of smaller vessels, many cargo ships, carrying land
'clads and infantry, gunboats and torpedo boats—virtually all the
remaining fighting ships of the nations of the world which had
taken part in the war.

If I had believed in the cause of the Ashanti Empire I am
sure I would have felt a surge of pride when I looked upon the
splendour of that fleet as it steamed away from Reykjavik in the
early morning of 23rd December, 1907—a mass of black and
scarlet upon the grey field of the wintry sea. Wisps of fog drifted
from time to time across the scene and, standing on the quarter-
deck of the *Dingiswayo*, listening to the sound of ships' horns
bellowing in the distance, I was overwhelmed with a sense of
awe. How, I wondered, could anything in the world resist such
might? And if there was a God, how could He allow it to have
been created in the first place?

It seemed to me, at that moment, that I had been torn from
my own world to witness a vision of Armageddon—and, oddly
enough, I felt privileged!

I think that it was then that the notion first occurred to me
that perhaps I had been selected by Providence to be involved
in a countless series of what might be called alternative versions
of the Apocalypse—that I was doomed to witness the end of the
world over and over again and doomed, too, to search for a world
where Man had learned to control the impulses which led to such
suicidal conflicts, perhaps never to find it. I still do not quite
understand my motives in recording my experiences, but it could
be that I hope that, if they are ever read, they will serve as a lesson
to a world which has so far managed to avert its own destruction.

But, as I have said before, I am neither introspective nor
morbid by nature, and my thoughts soon returned to the more
immediate aspects of my situation.

* * *

It was about 4 p.m. on Christmas Day, 1907, that the Australasian-Japanese fleet was sighted speeding rapidly from south-south-west out of the twilight, firing as it came.

Night had fallen by the time we properly engaged and the fighting was confused. The air was full of fire and noise. Above us the air fleets were locked in terrible conflict, while on every side huge guns poured forth destruction seemingly at random, and when, at sudden moments, there came a lull, when there was a second or two of silence and blackness, I experienced a cold and impossible fear, certain that it was all over, that the world itself had been destroyed and that the sun would never rise again.

By means of wireless telegraphy, Hood was able to direct the battle from the *Chaka*, which was riding somewhere above the clouds, and it became evident to me that he was building up a defensive position around the contents of that huge and mysterious hull at the centre of our fleet. The *Dingiswayo*, also close to the centre, was not therefore immediately engaged in battle, but impatiently awaited orders to have a crack at the enemy, firing occasionally, when so commanded, into the sky at one of the Australasian-Japanese airships, which would return our shots with bombs and concentrated cannon-fire, none of which happily scored a direct hit and all of which failed to pierce our super-strong steel armour.

At last we received an order to break formation and moved at full speed to a position on the starboard flank of the main Australasian-Japanese grouping, where our own ships were sustaining particularly heavy losses.

We seemed at first to be moving away from the main battle—away from the crimson and yellow flashes of the guns, the incessant booming, and into utter blackness. Then, suddenly, as if receiving warning of our presence, two battleships turned their searchlights on us. Powerful beams of white light struck us in the eyes and blinded us for the moment. I was still on the quarter-deck, with precious little to do, not being a regular officer of the ship. I heard the captain shouting from the bridge, saw our long guns begin to swing into position, felt the *Dingiswayo* roll as she turned at an acute angle, broadside to the enemy, giving me my first clear view of two long lines of battleships, some mere silhouettes in the darkness, and others speckled with reflected light from the gun-flashes to port. Then the air was full of the whine of shells, the chunky, throaty noise of those shells hitting the water ahead and astern of us, but never, thankfully, scoring on either our hull or superstructure. Then all our guns began to go off and the *Dingiswayo* shuddered from stem to stern so that I thought she might well shake herself to pieces. Our shells left the muzzles of the guns with a kind of high-pitched yell—almost an exultation—and the enemy ships were grouped so tightly together that we could not miss. The shells hit the battleships and exploded. Heavy smoke drifted back to us and we were all forced to don the special masks designed for the purpose of protecting our lungs in just such circumstances.

The air had been cold, the temperature well below zero, but now it began to heat up, becoming tropical, as far as we were concerned. We went about and sought the darkness again, knowing that we had been lucky and that we could not expect to take on a dozen or more battleships alone.

For a while the searchlights roamed across the sea, trying to pick us out, but we skulked just out of their range, using their own lights to try to get some idea of our best chance. A battleship had detached itself from the main formation and was rushing blindly towards us, apparently unaware of our presence in its path. It was a splendid opportunity for us. I heard the order given to release torpedoes but to hold off firing. There was a faint sound, like the striking of a bell, and the torpedoes sped silently towards their prey, darting from our tubes while the enemy ship remained unaware that she was under attack!

The torpedoes scored direct hits below the battleship's waterline. She was holed in five places and was sinking even before she realized it. I heard a confused shouting from her decks, and her searchlights came on, but already she was keeling over and the lights slowly rose into the sky like the fingers of a clutching, imploring hand. She went down without having fired a single shot. For a little while I saw her electrics gleaming below the surface, winking out slowly as she sank, and then the water was black again, dotted with a few bits of wreckage and a handful of wailing sailors.

There was no time to pick up survivors, even if we had wished to (and the Ashanti did not believe in showing much mercy to defeated enemies). We had been sighted again and two battleships were rushing towards us at speeds which would have seemed incredible on land and which were, to me, all but impossible on sea! We were capable of not much more than half their speed, but again we were successful in finding covering darkness.

It seemed to me that we had moved quite a long way off from the main conflict. At least a mile away now, the sea and the sky seemed to be one vast mass of flame, lighting a wide area and revealing wreck upon wreck. The entire sea was filled with broken remains—both of ordinary battleships and fallen airships—while beneath this mass of torn metal and blazing oil and wood could sometimes be seen the dark shapes of the underwater boats, like so many gigantic killer whales, seeking out fresh prey.

Once I had a glimpse of two subaquatic destroyers locked in conflict several fathoms below, searchlights piercing the gloom, guns flashing in what was to me an eery silence. Then one of the boats wheeled and dived deeper and the other followed it, still firing. I saw something flicker down there and then suddenly the water above the scene gushed up like a monstrous geyser, flinging fragments of metal and corpses high into the air, and I knew it was all over for one of the vessels.

My attention went back to the two battleships whose searchlights had picked us up. Our decks were suddenly flooded with light and almost immediately the enemy guns began to go off. This time we were not so lucky. An explosive shell hit us somewhere amidships and I was flung backwards by the force of the blast. A fire-fighting team ran past me, paying out a hose behind it, and I saw the fire flicker out in what must have been seconds. I pulled myself to my feet and climbed the companionway to the bridge, where the captain, peering through a pair of night-glasses, was rapping out orders through an electrical loud-hailer which amplified his clicking, harshly accented speech (it was an Ivory Coast dialect with which I was unfamiliar). Again the *Dingiswayo* went about, taking evasive action, all her port guns firing at once and scoring at least two hits on the vessel which had damaged us. We saw her lurch heavily over to one side and settle in the water, part of her hull glowing red-hot and a shower of sparks streaming into the air from a point near her afterbridge. We must have hit some vital part of her, for a moment later there came an awesome explosion which flung me backwards once again so that this time my spine struck the rail and winded me horribly. Oily black smoke was borne on the wind of the explosion and blinded us, and the *Dingiswayo* was buffeted as badly as if she had been seized suddenly by a hurricane, but then the smoke cleared and we saw little of the other ship, just something which might have been her top-mast standing out for a second above the waterline and then this, too, disappeared.

Her sister ship now commenced a heavy cannonade and again we were hit, though not badly, and were able to fire back until the enemy evidently thought better of continuing the engagement, turned about and sped at its maximum rate of knots back into the darkness.

This cautious action on the part of the enemy skipper had a considerable effect on our own morale and a huge cheer went up from our decks while our forward gun fired one last, contemptuous shot at the stern of the retreating vessel.

It seemed to me (and I was later proved correct) that for all its superiority of speed and fire-power, the Australasian-Japanese navy had little stomach for fighting. They had had no direct experience of naval warfare, whereas the Ashanti had been fighting now for several years and were used to risking death almost daily. Faced with the terrible implications of actual battle, our enemy began to lose its nerve. This was the pattern, also, above and below the waves.

But by dawn we were still fighting. For miles in all directions battleship met battleship, steering through a veritable Sargasso Sea of wreckage (in many places it was virtually impossible to see the water at all), and the air continued to be filled with the booming of the guns, the whine of the shells and, less audible but far more chilling to my ears, the screams and the wails of the wounded, the drowning, the abandoned of both sides. Parts of the water were on fire, sending sooty smoke into the cold, grey sky, and now the cloud had come down so low that it was rare to catch sight of an aerial ironclad as it manoeuvred overhead, though we could hear the guns sounding like thunder and see occasional flashes of light, like lightning, every so often split those clouds. A couple of times I saw a blazing hull fall suddenly from out of the grey, boiling canopy above us.

We were soon engaged again, with a ship called the *Iwo Shima*, which had already seen some pretty fierce fighting by the look of her. Part of her bows, above the waterline, had been blown away and there was a great pile of miscellaneous junk in her starboard scuppers which had either been washed or blown there by whatever had damaged her bridge. But she was plucky and she still had a considerable amount of fire-power, as she proved. I think she felt that she was doomed anyway, and was determined to take the *Dingiswayo* to the bottom with her, for she showed no concern for her own safety, steaming directly at us, apparently with the intention of ramming us full on if her guns didn't sink us first.

In the distance there were a hundred ships of varying tonnage locked in similar struggles, but I saw no sign of the great hull we had been protecting, nor of the ships which had been assigned to tow her, and it seemed to me then that she had gone down.

The *Iwo Shima* did not waver in her course and we were forced to do what we could to avoid her, giving her everything we had left from our forward guns and, for the first time, using every machine-gun that we had behind armour in the fighting tops. This manoeuvre brought us so close to the enemy that we almost touched and neither of us could use any of our big guns at such close range, nor risk using torpedoes. I got a good view of the Japanese seamen, their elaborate and somewhat unfunctional uniforms torn and dirty, their faces begrimed with blood, soot and sweat, watching us grimly as they sped past us, already beginning to turn in the hope of taking us in our stern. But we were turning, too, and a few minutes later the manoeuvre was all over. On our captain's orders, we released our starboard torpedoes the instant we were broadside of the *Iwo Shima*, at the same time pouring the last of our fire-power into her, every starboard gun firing at once. She was fast enough to escape most of what we sent, but her speed told against her, for her retaliatory fire went wide of us, scoring only one minor hit in our starboard bow. We had managed to upset most of the big guns in her battery, but she turned again, much slower now, for our torpedoes had damaged at least one of her screws. But now the sea had begun to rise, making it much more difficult to aim or, indeed, to see our enemy. Everywhere I looked there were walls of water containing all varieties of flotsam—metal, wood and flesh jostling together in some ghastly minuet—and then the sea would sink for a moment, revealing the *Iwo Shima*, and we would fire hastily until, momentarily, she disappeared again.

Our own damage was not slight. From somewhere below, our pumps were working full out to clear many of the compartments which were flooded. In several places the superstructure of the ship had fused into strange, jagged shapes, and corpses hung limply from damaged positions in the fighting tops, where medical staff had been unable to reach them. We had two big holes above the waterline and a smaller one below, amidships, and we had lost at least thirty men. In ordinary circumstances we might have retired with perfect honour, but all of us knew that this battle was crucial, and there was nothing for it but to fight on. We were closing on the *Iwo Shima* now, letting the sea carry us broadside on to the enemy ironclad, going about so that, with luck, we should be able to take her with our port battery which was in better condition and better equipped to deal with her.

We rose on the crest of a great wave and saw the *Iwo Shima* below us. She had taken in more water than her pumps could cope with and she was already beginning to list astern and to starboard. As the huge wave carried us down, we commenced firing.

The *Iwo Shima* went down without letting go another shot. The water foamed and hissed; and we saw her bows jutting stubbornly out of the green-grey ocean for a second or two and then she was gone. Immediately we went full astern, to avoid being dragged down by her undertow, and there came a massive, grumbling series of explosions from below, immediately followed by a roaring water-spout which shot at least a hundred feet into the air and rained our decks with tiny pieces of shrapnel.

Again, cheering broke out all over the ship, but was swiftly stifled as a heavy black shape emerged from the clouds overhead. The *Iwo Shima* must have signaled to one of her sister airships for help just before she went down. We had hardly anything left with which to defend ourselves. Machine-gunners in the fighting tops aimed their guns upwards, pouring round after round into the hull of the flying ironclad. I could hear a steady *ping ping* as our bullets struck metal, but they had about as much effect as a cloud of midges on a charging rhinoceros. It was our good fortune that this monster had evidently dropped all her bombs and spent her heavy artillery, for she answered us with a chatter of steam-gatlings, raking our decks where our men were thickest and wreaking immediate havoc so that in one moment where there had been proud, cheering individuals, citizens of the Ashanti Empire, there was now a horrible mass of writhing, bloody flesh.

I could read the name emblazoned on the airship's dark hull—the R.A.A. *Botany Bay*—and made out her insignia. This gave me a peculiar lurching sensation in the pit of my stomach, for she was flying the good old Union Jack inset with the crimson chrysanthemum of Imperial Japan! Half of me wanted to hail the ship as a friend, while the other half shared the emotions of my fellows aboard the *Dingiswayo* as they fought desperately and hopelessly back. Only our stern gun, a sort of latter-day Long Tom, was operational, and as the *Botany Bay* went past, we managed to get off three or four shots at her, holing her astern, just above her main propellers, but it was the best we could do. Apparently careless of the damage we had done to her, she made a graceful turn in the air and fell upon us again. This time I barely managed to get down behind the shield of one of our useless 9-inch guns before the bullets hailed across our decks.

When I next raised my head, I was fully expecting death, but saw instead the black-and-white markings of one of our own aerial cruisers, dropping down almost as if out of control, so swiftly did she move, clouds of grey smoke puffing from the length of her slender hull as she gave off a massive cannonade. Shell after shell struck the top of the *Botany Bay*'s armoured canopy, piercing it so that her buoyancy tanks were thoroughly holed. She turned first on one side and then on the other and it was a horrifying as well as an awe-inspiring sight to see such a huge beast rolling in the air almost directly above our heads! I have witnessed the death-agonies of more than one airship, but I have never seen anything quite like the death of the *Botany Bay*. She shuddered. She tried to right herself. She lost height and then shot into the air again, almost to the base of the clouds, then her nose dipped, her convulsions ceased and she smashed down into the sea, disappearing beneath the waves and bobbing up again on her side, steam hissing from her ports, to lie upon the face of the ocean like a dying whale. Few inside her could have survived that awful shaking and we made no attempt to discover if there were survivors. Our own flying cruiser dipped her tail to us by way of salute and climbed back into the clouds.

A few minutes later, as we moved among our wounded, trying to save those we could, news came over the wireless apparatus, telling us to rejoin the main fleet at a position which would put us only a few miles off the coast of Newfoundland. The Battle of the Atlantic was over, the enemy fleet having retired, but the Battle of America had not yet begun.

CHAPTER TWO

The Land Leviathan

What remained of our fleet regrouped the next morning. For all that we had defeated the Australasian-Japanese fleet, we had probably sustained greater losses. There were scarcely a dozen flying ironclads left, perhaps five underwater ships operational, and of the surface fleet half had been sunk, while most of the fifty or so surviving craft had all sustained damage, some of it crippling. The *Dingiswayo*, pumps still working full out, was perhaps in better condition than most of its sister craft, and the only ships to have received minimal damage were those which, under cover of the darkness, had towed the huge floating hull out of danger. I saw Hood's *Chaka* flying overhead, inspecting us as we rose and fell on a moderately heavy sea. A misty rain was falling, adding to the gloomy atmosphere permeating the whole fleet. Somehow the proud black-and-scarlet lion banners we flew did not look so splendid in the wintry, North Atlantic light as they had done under the blazing skies of Africa. Clad in heavy jerseys and sea-cloaks, our caps pulled well down to protect us from the worst of the drizzle, we stood on our decks, shivering, weary and pessimistic. Messages of approval began to come down from the *Chaka*, but could not break our mood. It was the first experience many of the Africans had had of real cold, the sort of cold which cuts into the marrow and threatens to freeze the blood, and liberal amounts of hot toddy seemed to have no effect at all against the weather.

I was standing on the bridge, discussing the conditions with the skipper, Captain Ombuto, who was dismayed to learn that temperatures seemed to me to be somewhat high for the time of year, when a message came through from the *Chaka* which directly concerned me. He read the message, raising his eyebrows and handing it to me. A decent sort, Captain Ombuto had shown me none of the prejudice I had experienced from some of his brother officers. He spoke English with a strong French accent (he had served for a while in the Arabian navy before the war). "The top brass seems concerned for your safety, Bastable."

The message was unsigned, save with the name of the flagship, and read: "Urgent you give details of officers killed and wounded. How is Bastable? Report immediately." The message was in English, although French was also used, pretty indiscriminately, as the *lingua franca* of Ashanti.

Captain Ombuto waited until he had a full list of his dead and wounded before relaying the details to the flagship, adding: "Bastable unharmed" at the end of his reply. A little later there came a second message: "Please relay my sympathy to those who lost so many comrades. You fought well and honourably. Send Bastable to flagship. Boat coming." It was signed simply "Hood". Ombuto read the message aloud to me, shrugged and removed his cap, scratching his head. "Until now Mrs. Persson has been the only member of your race allowed aboard the flagship. You're going up in the world, Bastable." He jerked his thumb in the air. "Quite literally, eh!"

A short while later an airboat landed on the crippled deck of the *Dingiswayo* and I climbed into it, returning the smart salute of the shivering officer of the Lion Guard who commanded it. The poor man looked wretched and I reflected a little cynically that if Hood intended to drive through America into the Southern States, his men could not have a better incentive than the promise of warmer weather!

Twenty minutes later the airboat had entered the huge stern hatches of the *Chaka* and come to rest in the specially modified hangar adapted from the two lowest decks. An electric lift bore us upwards into the depths of the massive ship and soon I stood with my feet in the soft, scarlet plush of the control room carpet. The control room had windows all around it, but they did not look out from the ship but into its interior. From the windows could be seen the main battle-deck, the big guns jutting through their portholes, the bomb bays (mostly empty now) and the war-weary officers and men standing by their positions. General Hood had had, by the look of him, even less sleep than I, but Una Persson seemed extraordinarily fresh. It was she who greeted me first.

"Good morning, Mr. Bastable. Congratulations on surviving the battle!"

General Hood said, half-proudly, "It was probably the fiercest and biggest sea-battle in the history of the world. And we won it, Mr. Bastable. What do you think of us now? Are we still nothing more than barbarians who pick upon the weak and innocent, the wounded and the defenseless?"

"Your men and your ships acquitted themselves with great bravery and considerable skill," I admitted. "And in this case I would say they had everything to be proud of—for the

Australasian-Japanese fleet attacked us, without even bothering to parley."

"Us?" Hood was quick to pick up the word. "So you identify with our cause, after all."

"I identified with my ship," I said, "for all that I had precious little to do aboard her. Still, I gather I am here as an observer, not a participant."

"That is up to you, Mr. Bastable," retorted Hood, running his black hands through his greying hair. "I have merely given you the opportunity to make your choice! We are about to have luncheon. Won't you join us?"

I made a stiff little bow. "Thank you," I said.

"Then, come." He linked his arm in mine and ushered me from the control room into his private quarters, which were linked to the bridge by a short companionway leading directly into his cabin. Here lunch had already been laid out—an excellent selection of cold food which I could not resist. A fine hock was served and I accepted a glass readily.

"Conditions aboard airships seem rather better than those on ordinary ships," I said. "It's freezing down there, almost impossible to get warm unless you're actually in the boiler-room. At least an old-fashioned ironclad, powered by coal, heated up in almost any temperature!"

"Well, we'll be making landfall by tomorrow," said Hood dismissively as he ate. "However, if you would be more comfortable aboard the *Chaka* I would be glad to have you as my guest."

I was about to reject his invitation when Una Persson, seated beside me and wearing a long, simple gown of brown velvet, put a hand on my arm. "Please stay, Mr. Bastable. It will give you a better chance to witness the invasion of New York."

"Does New York *require* invading? I had heard that there is hardly anyone living there now."

"A few thousand," said Hood airily. "And about a third of those will doubtless join us when we arrive."

"How can you be sure of that?" I asked.

"My agents have been active, Mr. Bastable. You forget that I have retained contacts all over the United States—it is my home country…"

If I had entertained any doubts concerning Hood's ability to attack and take the city of New York, they were quickly dispersed upon our arrival in what had been one of the largest and richest harbours in the world. New York had sustained if anything a heavier bombardment than London. She had been famous for her tall, metallic towers which had gleamed with a thousand bright colours, but now only two or three of those towers were left standing, stained by the elements, ravaged by explosions, threatening to collapse into the rubble which completely obscured any sign of where her broad avenues, her shady, tree-lined streets, her many parks had stood. A cold wind swept the ruins as our ships came to anchor and our aircraft began to spread out in formation, scouting for any signs of resistance. The *Chaka* made several flights over New York, dropping sometimes to a height of fifty feet. There were plenty of signs that these ruins were inhabited. Large fires burned in the hollows formed by tumbled concrete slabs, groups of ragged men and women ran for cover as the shadow of our great craft touched them, while others merely stood and gaped.

Elsewhere I had the impression that some form of order existed. I thought I glimpsed dirty white uniforms—soldiers wearing what might have been helmets which obscured their faces. No shots were fired at us, however, by the small groups which hastily made for the shadows whenever we approached.

The scene was made even more desolate by the presence of great drifts of snow, much of it dirty and half-melted, everywhere.

"I see hardly any point in bothering to take the place," I said to General Hood.

He frowned at this. "It is a question of destroying the morale of any defenders—here or in other parts of the country," he said. There was an expression of almost fanatical intensity on his black features and his eyes never left the ruins. From time to time he would say, with a mixture of nostalgia and satisfaction, that this was where he had had his first flat in New York; there was where he had worked for one summer as a student; that the heap of rusting girders and shattered stone over which we flew was some famous museum or office building. It was not pleasant to hear him speaking thus—a sort of litany of gloating triumph. Slightly sickened, I turned away from the observation window, and saw Una Persson standing behind us, a look of quizzical and yet tender melancholy on her face, as if she, in her way, also regretted having to listen to Cicero Hood's morbidly gleeful remarks.

"It will be nightfall in three hours," she said. "Perhaps it would be best to wait until morning before making the landing?"

He turned, almost angry. "No! We land now. I'll give the command. Let them see my power!" He reached for a speaking-tube, barking orders into it. "Prepare for landing! Any resistance to be met without mercy. Tonight the Ashanti celebrate. Let the men have whatever spoils they can find. Contact our friends here. Bring the leaders to me as soon as they have revealed themselves. Tomorrow we continue towards Washington!"

It was with pity that I returned my attention to the ruins. "Could you not spare them?" I asked him. "Have they not suffered too much?"

"Not from me, Mr. Bastable." His voice was savage. "Not from me!"

He refused to continue any sort of conversation, waving a dismissive hand both at Una Persson and myself. "If you cannot share my pleasure, then pray do not try to spoil it for me! Go, both of you. I want no whites here!"

Una Persson was plainly hurt, but she did not remonstrate. She left when I left and we went together to another observation deck, forward, where we probably had a better view of the landing.

First came the infantry, brought ashore in the boats and lining up in orderly ranks on what remained of the quays. Next, huge ramps were extended from the ships and from out of their bowels began to rumble the great armour-plated "land ironclads". It hardly seemed possible that so many of the cumbersome machines could have been contained even in that large fleet. Rolling over every obstacle, they manoeuvred into wedge-shaped formations, all facing inland, their top-turrets swinging round to threaten New York with their long guns, their lower turrets rotating slowly as their crews ran a series of tests to make sure they were in perfect working order. Although the Ashanti had lost about half their force during the Battle of the Atlantic, they could still field a good-sized army and it was doubtful if the United States, crushed by the terrible War Between the Nations, could find anything likely to withstand them. The U.S.A. must now depend on the Australasian-Japanese Federation for support (and we all were sure that they would make some new attempt to stop General Hood).

But now at last I was to see what had been hidden in that gigantic hull which we had towed all the way from Africa. And Una Persson's expression became eager as the hull was towed into position against the dockside.

"This is the result of what I was able to find in England, Mr. Bastable," she said in an excited murmur. "An invention of O'Bean's that was regarded as too terrible ever to put into production, even at the height of the war. Watch!"

I watched, as the dusk began to gather. From somewhere

inside the hull bolts were withdrawn, releasing the sides so that they fell backwards into the sea and forwards onto the dock. One by one the sections swung down until the contents of the hull were revealed. It was a ziggurat of steel. Tier upon tier it rose, utterly dwarfing the assembled machines which had already landed. From each tier there jutted guns which put to shame anything we had had on the *Dingiswayo*. On the top-most turret (the smallest on this metal pyramid) were mounted four long-snouted guns, on the second turret down there were six such guns, on the third there were twelve, on the fourth there were eighteen. On the fifth tier could be seen banks of smaller guns, perhaps a third of the size of the others, for use in close-range fire. There were about thirty of these. On the sixth tier down were some fifty similar guns, while in the seventh and bottom-most tier were upwards of a hundred of the most modern steam-gatlings, each capable of firing 150 rounds a minute. There were also slits in the armour plating all the way up, for riflemen. There were grilled observation ports in every tier, and each turret was capable of swiveling independently of the others, just as each gun was capable of a wide range of movement within the turret. The whole thing was mounted on massive wheels, the smallest of these wheels being at least four times the height of a man, mounted (I learned later) on separate chassis in groups of ten, which meant that the vast machine could move forwards, backwards or *sideways* whenever it wished. Moreover, the size of the wheels and the weight they carried could crush almost any obstacle.

This was General Hood's 'secret weapon'. It must have taken half the wealth of Africa and Europe combined to build it. There had never been any moving thing of its size in the world before (and precious few non-mobile things!). With it, I felt sure, the Black Attila was invincible. No wonder he had been prepared to sacrifice the rest of his invasion fleet in order to protect it!

This was truly a symbol of the Final War, of Armageddon!

A leviathan released upon the land—a monster capable of destroying anything in its path—a steel-clad, gargantuan dragon bringing roaring death to all who resisted. Its gleaming, blue-grey hull displayed on four sides of each of its tiers the scarlet circle framing the black, rampant lion of Ashanti, symbol of a powerful, vengeful Africa—of an Africa which remembered the millions of black slaves who had been crowded into stinking, disease-ridden hulks to serve the White Dream—of an Africa which had waited for its moment to release this invulnerable creature upon the offspring of those who had tortured its peoples, insulted them, killed them, terrified them and robbed them over the centuries.

If justice it was, then it was to be a fearful and a spectacular justice indeed!

As I watched the Land Leviathan roll through concrete and steel as easily as one might crush grass beneath one's feet, I thought not merely of the fate which was about to befall America, but what might happen to the rest of the world, particularly Bantustan, when Hood had realized his plans here.

Having created such a beast, it seemed to me, he would have to go on using it. Ultimately it must become the master, conquering the conqueror, until nothing of the world survived at all!

Certainly that had been the logic of this world up to now and I saw nothing—save perhaps the ideal that was the country of Bantustan—to deny that logic.

I felt then that it was my moral duty to do anything I could to stop Hood's terrible pattern of conquest, but the assassination of one man no longer seemed the answer. In a quandary I turned away from the scene as night fell and the lights of the Land Leviathan pierced the darkness like so many fearsome eyes.

Mrs. Persson said something to me, but I did not hear her. I stumbled from the observation deck, my mind in complete confusion, certain that she and I might well be, in a short while, the last surviving members of our race.

CHAPTER THREE

The Deserter

It took five hours to crush New York. And "crush" is quite literally the proper description. Hood's monstrous machine rolled at will through the ruins, pushing down the few towers which remained standing, firing brief, totally destructive, barrages into the positions of those who resisted. All the Negroes in New York, who had been fighting the whites well before we arrived, rallied at once to Hood's black-and-scarlet banner, and by noon the few defenders who remained alive were rounded up and interrogated for the information they could supply concerning other pockets of "resistance" across the country.

Hood invited me to be present at one of these questionings and I accepted, hoping only that I could put in a plea for mercy for the poor devils who had fallen into Ashanti hands.

Hood was now dressed in a splendid military uniform—also black and scarlet, but with a considerable quantity of gold and silver braid and a three-cornered hat sporting the same ostrich plumes as his "Lion Guard". Hood had confided to me that such *braggadocio* was completely against his instincts, but that he was expected to affect the proper style both by his enemies and by those who followed him. He had a curved sword almost permanently in his right hand, and stuck into his belt, unholstered, were two large, long-barreled automatic pistols, rather like Mausers. The prisoners were being questioned in what remained of the cellar of a house which had stood on Washington Square. They were wounded, half-starved, filthy and frightened. Their white hoods (there was some superstition which had grown up that these hoods protected them from the plague) had been torn from their heads and their uniforms, crudely fashioned from flour sacks, were torn and blood-stained. I did not, I must admit, feel any pride in these representatives of my own race. They would have been gutter-rats no matter what conditions prevailed in New York and doubtless it was because they were gutter-rats that they had managed to survive, with the ferocity and tenacity of their kind. They were spitting, snarling, shrieking at their Ashanti conquerors and their language was the foulest I have ever heard. Una Persson stood nearby and I would have given anything in the world for her not to have been subjected to that disgusting swearing.

The man who seemed to be the leader of the group (he had conferred upon himself the title of Governor!) had the surname of Hoover and his companions referred to him as "Speed". He was a typical example of that breed of New York small-time 'crooks' who are ready to take up any form of crime so long as there is little chance of being caught. It was written all over his mean, ugly, hate-filled face. Doubtless, before he elected himself "Governor", he had contented himself with robbing the weak and the helpless, of frightening children and old folk, and running errands for the larger, more successful 'gang bosses' of the city. Yet I felt a certain sympathy for him as he continued to rant and rave, turning his attention at last upon me.

"As fer yer, ya nigger-lover, yore nuttin' but a dirty traitor!" was the only repeatable statement of this kind that he made. He spat at me, then turned on the mild-faced lieutenant (I think he was called Azuma) who had been questioning him. "We knew you niggers wuz comin'—we bin hearin' 'bout it fer months now—an' dey're gettin' ready fer yer. Dey got plans—dey got a way o' stoppin' yer real good!" He sniggered. "Yer got der artillery—but yer ain't got der brains, see? Yer'll soon be t'rowin' in der sponge. It'll take more'n what *you* got ter lick real white men!"

His threats, however, were all vague, and it soon became obvious to Lieutenant Azuma that there was little point in continuing with his questions.

I had not taken kindly to being called a traitor by this riff-raff, yet there was, I suppose, some truth in what he had said. I had not lifted my voice, let alone a finger, to try to stop Hood so far.

Now I said: "I must ask you, General Hood, to spare these men's lives. They are prisoners of war, after all."

Hood exchanged a look of cruel amusement with Lieutenant Azuma. "But surely they are hardly worth sparing, Mr. Bastable," he said. "What use would such as these be in any kind of society?"

"They have a right to their lives," I said.

"They would scarcely agree with you if you were speaking up for *me*," said Cicero Hood coldly now. "You heard Hoover's remark about 'niggers'. If our situation were reversed, do you think your pleas would be heard?"

"No," I said. "But if you are to prove yourself better than such as Hoover, then you must set an example."

"That is your Western morality, again," said Hood. Then he laughed, without much humour. "But we had no intention of killing them. They will be left behind in the charge of our friends. They will help in the rebuilding of New Benin, as the city is to be called henceforth."

With that, he strode from the cellar, still laughing that peculiar, blood-chilling laugh.

* * *

And so Hood's land fleet rolled away from New York, and now I was a passenger in one of the smaller fighting machines. Our next objective was Philadelphia, where again Hood was, in his terms, going to the relief of the blacks there. The situation for the Negro in the America of this day was, I was forced to admit, a poor one. The whites, in seeking a scapegoat for their plight, had fixed, once again, upon the blacks. The other superstitious reason that so many of them wore those strange hoods was because they had conceived the idea that the Negroes were somehow 'dirtier' than the whites and that they had been responsible for spreading the plagues which had followed the war, as they had followed it in England. In many parts of the United States, members of the Negro race were being hunted like animals and burned alive when they were caught—the rationale for this disgusting behaviour being that it was the only way to be sure that the plague did not spread. For some reason Negroes had not been so vulnerable to the various germs contained in the bombs and it had been an easy step in the insane logic of the whites to see the black people, therefore, as 'carriers'. For two years or more, black groups had been organizing themselves, under instructions from Hood's agents, awaiting the day when the Ashanti invaded. Hood's claim that he was 'liberating' the blacks was, admittedly, not entirely unfounded in truth.

Nonetheless I did not feel that any of this was sufficient to vindicate Hood.

Headed by the Land Leviathan, the conquering army looted and burned its way through the states of New York, New Jersey and Pennsylvania, and wherever it paused it set up its black-and-scarlet banners, leaving local bands of Negroes behind to administer the conquered territories.

It was during the battle in which Philadelphia was completely destroyed, and every white man, woman and child slain by the pounding guns of the Land Leviathan, that I found my opportunity to 'desert' the Black Horde, first falling back from the convoy of which my armoured carriage was part, and then having the luck to capture a stray horse.

My intention was to head for Washington and warn the defenders there of what they might expect. Also, if possible, I wished to discuss methods of crippling the Land Leviathan. My only plan was that the monster should somehow be lured close to a cliff-top and fall over, smashing itself to pieces. How this could be achieved, I had not the slightest idea!

My ride from Philadelphia to the city of Wilmington probably set something of a record. Across the countryside groups of black 'soldiers' were in conflict with whites. In my Ashanti uniform, I was prey to both sides and would doubtless have fared worst at the hands of the whites who regarded me as a traitor than at the hands of the blacks, if I had been caught. But, by good fortune, I avoided capture until I rode into Wilmington, which had not suffered much bombing and merely had the deserted, overgrown look of so many of America's 'ghost cities'. On the outskirts, I stripped off my black tunic and threw it away—though the weather was still very cold—and dressed only in my singlet and britches—dismounted from my horse and searched for the local white leader.

They found me first. I was moving cautiously along one of the main thoroughfares when they suddenly appeared on all sides, wearing the sinister white hoods so reminiscent of those old Knights of the South, the Ku-Klux-Klan, whose fictional adventures had thrilled me as a boy. They asked me who and what I was and what I wanted in Wilmington. I told them that it was urgent that I should meet their leader, that I had crucial news of the Black Attila.

Shortly I found myself in a large civic building which a man named 'Bomber' Joe Kennedy was using as his headquarters. He had got his nickname, I learned later, from his skill in manufacturing explosive devices from a wide variety of materials. Kennedy had heard about me and it was only with the greatest self-restraint that he did not shoot me on the spot there and then—but he listened and he listened attentively and eventually he seemed satisfied that I was telling the truth. He informed me that he had already planned to take his small 'army' to Washington, to add it to the growing strength of the defenders. It would do no harm, he said, if I came with them, but he warned me that if at any time it seemed that I was actually spying for Hood I would be killed in the same way that Negroes were killed in those parts. I never found out what he meant and my only clue, when I enquired, was in the phrase which a grinning member of Kennedy's army quoted with relish. "Ever heard of 'burn or cut' in England, boy?" he asked me.

The whites had managed to build up the old railroad system, for most of the lines had survived the war and the locomotives were still functional, burning wood rather than coal these days. It was Kennedy's plan to transport himself and his army by rail to Washington (for there was a direct line), and the next day we climbed aboard the big, old-fashioned train, with myself and Kennedy joining the driver and fireman on the footplate, for, as Kennedy told me, "I don't wanna risk not keepin' you under my sight."

The train soon had a good head of steam and was rolling away from Wilmington in no time, its first stop being Baltimore, where Kennedy hoped to pick up a larger force of men.

As we rushed through the devastated countryside, Kennedy confided in me something of his life. He claimed that he had once been a very rich man, a millionaire, before the collapse. His family had come from Ireland originally and he had no liking for the English, whom he was inclined to rate second only to 'coons' as being responsible for the world's ills. It struck me as ironic that Kennedy should have a romantic attachment to one oppressed minority (as he saw it), but feel nothing but loathing for another.

Kennedy also told me that they were already making plans in Washington to resist the Black Attila. "They've got something up their sleeves which'll stop *him* in his tracks," he said smugly, but he would not amplify the statement and I had the impression that he was not altogether sure what the plan was.

Kennedy had also heard that there was a strong chance that the Washington 'army' would receive reinforcements from the Australasian-Japanese fleet which, he had it on good authority, had already anchored off Chesapeake Bay. I expressed the doubt that anything could withstand the Black Attila's Land Leviathan, but Kennedy was undaunted. He rubbed his nose and told me that there was "more than one way of skinnin' a coon".

Twice the train had to stop to take on more wood, but we were getting closer and closer to Baltimore and the city was little more than an hour away when a squadron of land ironclads appeared ahead of us, firing at the train. They flew the lion banner of Ashanti and must have gone ahead of the main army (perhaps having received intelligence that trains of white troops were on their way to Washington). I saw the long guns in their main turrets puff red fire and white smoke and a number of shells hit the ground close by. The driver was for putting on the brakes and surrendering, feeling that we did not have a chance, but Kennedy, for all that he might have been a cruel, ignorant and stupid man, was not a coward. He sent the word back along the train to get whatever big guns they could working, then he told the engineer to give the old locomotive all the speed she could take, and drove straight towards the lumbering war machines which were now on both sides of the track, positioned on the steep banks so that they could fire down at us as we passed.

I was reminded of an old print I once saw—a poster, I think, for Buffalo Bill's Wild West Show—of Red Indians attacking a train. The land ironclads were able to match our speed (for the train was carrying a huge number of cars), and their turrets could swing rapidly to shoot at us from any angle. Shell after shell began to smash into the train, but still she kept going, making for the safety of a long tunnel ahead of us, where the land 'clads could not follow.

We reached the tunnel with some relief and the engineer was for slowing down and stopping in the middle in the hope that the enemy machines would give up their chase, but Kennedy considered this a foolish scheme.

"They'll come at us from both ends, man!" he said. "They'll burrow through from the roof—they've got those 'mole' things which can bore through anything. We'll be like trapped rabbits down a hole if we stay here." I think there was sense to what he said, though our chances in the open were scarcely any better. Still, under his orders, the train raced on, breaking through into daylight to find half-a-dozen land ironclads waiting for it, their guns aimed at the mouth of the tunnel. How the locomotive survived that fusillade I shall never know, but survive it did, with part of the roof and a funnel shot away and its tender of wood blazing from the effects of a direct hit by an incendiary shell.

The rest of the train, however, was not so lucky.

A shell cut the coupling attaching us to the main part of the train and we lurched forward at a speed which threatened to hurl us from the tracks. Without the burden of the rest of the train, we were soon able to leave the ironclads behind. I looked back to see the stranded 'army' fighting it out with the armoured battleships of the land. They were being pounded to pieces.

Then we had turned a bend and left the scene behind. Kennedy looked crestfallen for a moment, and then he shrugged. There was little that could be done.

"Ah, well," he said. "We'll not be stopping in Baltimore now."

CHAPTER FOUR

The Triumphant Beast

Washington, surprisingly, had not sustained anything like the damage done to cities like New York and London. The government and all its departments had fled the capital before the war had got into its stride and had retired to an underground retreat somewhere in the Appalachians. It had survived the explosives, but not the plagues. Having little strategic importance, therefore, Washington had most of its famous buildings and monuments still standing. These overblown mock-Graecian, mock-Georgian tributes to grandiose bad taste could be seen in the distance as we steamed into the outskirts of the city, to be stopped by recently constructed barriers. These barriers had existed for only a week or so, but I was surprised at their solidity. They were of brick, stone and concrete, reinforced by neatly piled sand-bags, and, I gathered, protected the whole of the inner city. Kennedy's credentials were in order—he was recognized by three of the guards and welcomed as something of a hero—and we were allowed to continue through to the main railroad station, where he handed our locomotive over to the authorities. We were escorted through the wide, rather characterless streets (the famous trees had all been cut down in the making of the barriers and for fuel to power the trains) to the White House, occupied now by 'President' Beesley, a man who had once been a distinguished diplomat in the service of his country, but who had quickly profited from the hysteria following the war—he was believed to have been the first person to 'don the White Hood'. Beesley was fat and his red face bore all the earmarks of depravity. We were ushered into a study full of fine old 'colonial'-style furniture which gave the impression that nothing had changed since the old days. The only difference was in the smell and in the man sprawled in a large armchair at a desk near the bay window. The smell would have been regarded as offensive even in one of our own East End public houses—a mixture of alcohol, tobacco-smoke and human perspiration. Dressed in the full uniform of an American general, with the buttons straining to keep his tunic in place over his huge paunch, 'President' Beesley waved a hand holding a cigar by way of greeting, gestured with the other hand, which held a glass, for us to be seated. "I'm glad you could make it, Joe," he said to Kennedy, who seemed to be a close acquaintance. "Have a drink. Help yourself." He ignored me.

Kennedy went to a sideboard and poured himself a large glass of bourbon. "I'm sorry I couldn't bring you any men," he said. "You heard, did you, Ben? We got hit by a big fleet of that nigger's land 'clads. We were lucky to get through at all."

"I heard." Beesley turned small, cold eyes on me. "And that is the traitor, is it?"

"I had better tell you now," I said, though suddenly I was reluctant to justify myself, "that I joined Cicero Hood's entourage with the express purpose of trying to put a stop to his activities."

"And how did you intend to do that, Mr. Bastable?" said Beesley, leaning forward and winking at Kennedy.

"My original plan was to assassinate him," I said simply.

"But you didn't."

"After the Land Leviathan made its appearance I saw that killing Hood would do no good. He is the only one who has any control at all over the Black Horde. To kill him would have resulted in making things worse for you and all the other Europeans."

Beesley sniffed skeptically and sipped his drink, adding: "And what proof have we got of all this? What proof is there that you're not still working for Hood, that you're not planning to kill *me*?"

"None," I said. "But I want to discuss ways of stopping the Land Leviathan," I told him. "Those walls you're building will stop that monster no more than would paper. If we can dig some kind of deep trench—lay a trap like a gigantic animal trap—we might be able to put it out of action for a while at least…"

But President Beesley was smirking and shaking his head.

"We're ahead of you, Mr. Bastable. There's more than one kind of wall, you know. You've only seen what you might call our first line of defense."

"There isn't anything made strong enough to stop the Land Leviathan," I said emphatically.

"Oh, I don't know." Beesley gave Kennedy another of his secret looks. "Do you want to show him around, Joe? I think we can trust him. He's one of us."

Kennedy was not so certain. "Well, if you think so…"

"Sure I do. I have my hunches. He's okay. A bit misguided, a bit short on imagination—a bit English, eh? But a decent sort. Welcome to Washington, Mr. Bastable. Now you'll see how that black scum is to be stopped."

A while later we left the White House in a horse-drawn carriage provided for us. Kennedy, with some pride, explained how the Capitol had been turned into a well-defended arsenal and how every one of those overblown neo-Graecian buildings contained virtually every operational big gun left in the United States.

But it was not the architecture or the details of the defense system which arrested my vision—it was what I saw in the streets as I passed. Washington had always had a very large Negro population, and now this population was being put to use by the whites. I saw gangs of exhausted, half-starved men, women and children, shackled to one another by chains about the neck, wrists or ankles, hauling huge loads of bricks and sand-bags to the barricades. It was a scene from the past—with sweating, dying black slaves being worked, quite literally, to death by brutal white overseers armed with long bull-whips which they used liberally and with evident relish. It was a sight I had never expected to witness in the twentieth century! I was horrified, but did my best not to betray my emotion to Kennedy, who had not appeared to notice what was going on!

More than once I winced and was sickened when I saw some poor, near-naked woman fall and receive a torrent of abuse, kicked and whipped until she was forced to her feet again, or helped to her feet by her companions. Once I saw a half-grown boy collapse and it was quite plain that he was dead, but his fellow slaves were made to drag his corpse with them by the chains which secured his wrists to theirs.

Trying to appear insouciant, I said as coolly as I could: "I see now how you managed to raise the walls so quickly. You have reintroduced slavery."

"Well, you could call it that, couldn't you?" Kennedy grinned. "The blacks are performing a public service, like the rest of us, helping to build up the country again. Besides," and his face became serious, "it's what they know best. It's what most of 'em prefer. They don't think and feel the same as us, Bastable. It's like your worker bee—stop him from working and he becomes morbid and unhappy. Eventually he dies. It's the same with the blacks."

"Their ultimate fate would seem to be identical, however you look at it," I commented.

"Sure, but this way they're doing some good."

I must have seen several thousand Negroes as we traveled through the streets of Washington. A few were evidently employed as individual servants and were in a somewhat better position than their fellows, but most were chained together in gangs, sweating copiously for all that the weather was chill. There was little hope on any of their faces and I was not proud of my own race when I looked at them; also I could not help recalling the pride—arrogance, some would call it—in the bearing of Hood's Ashanti troops.

I stifled the thought, at that moment, but it kept coming back to me with greater and greater force. It was unjust to enslave other human beings and cruel to treat them in such a manner, whichever side committed the injustice. Yet it seemed to me that there was a grain more justice in Hood's policies—for he was repaying a debt, whereas men such as Beesley and Kennedy were acting from the most brutal and cynical of motives.

Mildly, I said: "But isn't it poor economics to work them so hard? They'll give you better value if they're treated a little better."

"That logic led to the Civil War, Mr. Bastable," said Kennedy, as if speaking to a child. "You start thinking like that and sooner or later they decide *they* deserve to be treated like white men and you get the old social ills being repeated over again. Besides," he grinned broadly, "there's not a lot of point in worrying too much about the life expectancy of our Washington niggers, as you'll see."

We were driving close to one of the main walls now. Here, as everywhere, huge gangs of Negroes were being forced to work at inhuman speed. It was no longer any mystery how Washington had managed to get its defenses up so rapidly. I tried to recall the stories of what Hood had done to the whites in Scandinavia, but even the stories, exaggerated and encouraged by Hood himself to improve his savage image, paled in comparison to the reality of what was happening in modern-day Washington!

As we passed the walls, I noticed that large cages, rather like the cages used for transporting circus animals about the country, were much in evidence on top of the walls. I pointed them out and asked Kennedy what they were.

He smirked as he leaned back in the carriage and lit a cigar. "*They*, Mr. Bastable, are our secret weapon."

I did not ask him to amplify this statement. I had become too saddened by the fate of the Negroes. I told Kennedy that I was tired and would like to rest. The carriage was turned about and I was taken to a hotel quite close to the Capitol, where I was given a room overlooking a stretch of parkland.

But even here I could look out through my windows and see evidence of the brutality of the whites. Not a hundred yards away, a pit of quick-lime had been sunk, and into it, from time to time, carts would dump the bodies of the dead and the dying.

I thought that I had witnessed Hell in Southern England, but now I knew that I had only been standing on the outskirts. Here, where it had once been declared an article of faith that all men were created equal, where it had seemed possible for the eighteenth-century ideals of reason and justice to be made reality, here was Hell, indeed!

And it was a hell created in the name of my own race, whose survival I hoped to ensure with my resistance to Hood and his Black Horde.

I slept badly at the hotel and the next morning sought an interview with 'President' Beesley at the White House. I received word that he was too busy to see me. I wandered about the streets, but there was too much there to turn my stomach. I began to feel angry. I felt frustrated. I wanted to remonstrate with Beesley, to beg him to show mercy to the blacks, to set an example of tolerance and decency to his white-hooded followers. Gandhi had been right. There was only one way to behave, even if it seemed, in the short term, against one's self-interest. Surely it was in one's self-interest in the long term to exhibit generosity, humanity, kindness and a sense of justice to one's fellow men. It was cynicism of Beesley's kind which had, after all, led to the threatened extinction of the whole human race. There could be no such thing as a 'righteous' war, for war was by its very nature an act of injustice against the individual, but there could be such a thing as an 'unrighteous' war—an evil war, a war begun by men who were utterly corrupt, both morally and intellectually. I had begun to think that it was a definition of those who would make war—that whatever motives they claimed, whatever ideals they promoted, whatever 'threat' they referred to, they could not be excused—because of their actions they could only be of a degenerate and immoral character.

Gandhi had said that violence bred violence. Well, it seemed that I was witnessing a living lesson in this creed! I realized how close I had, myself, been to the brink of behaving brutally and cynically, when I had contemplated the assassination of Hood.

Once again, at about the worst time possible, I found my loyalties divided, my mind in confusion, filled with a sense of the impossibility of any action whatsoever on my own part.

I had wandered away from the main roads of Washington and into a series of residential streets full of those fine terraced houses reminiscent of our own Regency squares and crescents. The houses, however, were much run-down. In most cases there was no glass in the windows and many doors showed signs of having been forced. I guessed that there had been fighting here, not by an invading army, but between the Negroes and the whites.

I was speculating, again, on the nature of the animal cages placed along the walls of the city, when I turned a corner and was confronted with a long line of black workers, chained ankle to ankle, shuffling along the centre of the road and pulling a big, wheeled platform on which had been piled a tottering mountain of sand-bags. There was hardly one of these people who was not bleeding from the cuts of the long whips wielded by armed overseers. Many seemed hardly capable of putting one foot in front of the other. They seemed destined, very shortly, for the lime-pits—and yet they were singing. They were singing as the Christian martyrs had been said to sing on their way to the Roman arena. They were singing a dirge of which it was difficult to distinguish the words at first. The white men, clad in heavy hoods, were yelling at them to stop. Their voices were muffled, but their whips were eloquent. But still the Negroes sang and now I made out some of the words.

> "He will come—*he will come*—
> Out of Africa—*he will come*—
> He will ride the Beast—*he will come*—
> He will set us free—*he will come*—
> He will bring us Pride—*he will come*—"

There was no question, of course, that the song referred to Hood and that it was being sung deliberately to incense the whites. The refrain was being sung by a tall, handsome young man who somehow managed to lift his head and keep his shoulders straight no matter how many savage blows fell upon him. His dignity and his courage were so greatly in contrast to the hysterical and cowardly actions of the whites that it was impossible to feel anything but admiration for him.

But I think that the gang of slaves was doomed. They would not stop singing and now, ominously, the hooded whites lowered their whips and began to take their guns from their shoulders.

The procession stopped.

The voices stopped.

The first white ripped off his hood and revealed a hate-filled face which could have seen no more than seventeen summers. He raised his weapon to his shoulders, grinning.

"Okay—you wanna go on singing?"

The tall Negro took a breath, knowing that it was probably his last, and began the first words of the chant.

That was when, impulsively, I dived for the boy, throwing my whole weight against him so that his shot went into the air. I had grabbed the gun even as I fell on top of him. I heard confused shouts and then heard the sharp report of another rifle. I saw a bullet strike the body of the boy and I used that body as cover, shooting back at my fellow whites!

I should not have lasted long, of course, had not the tall Negro uttered a bellow which was almost gleeful and led his companions upon the whites, who had their backs to the blacks while they concentrated on me.

I saw white hoods bobbing for a moment in a sea of black, blistered flesh. I heard a few shots fired and then it was over. The whites lay dead upon the pavement and the blacks were using their guns to shoot themselves free of the chains on their legs. I was not sure how I would be received and I stood up cautiously, ready to run if necessary, for I knew that many Negroes felt little sentimentality to whites, even if those whites were not directly involved in harming them.

Then the black youth grinned at me. "Thanks, mister. Why ain't you wearing your hood?"

"I have never worn one," I told him. "I'm British."

I suppose I must have sounded a little pompous, for the youth laughed aloud at this, before saying: "We'd better get off the streets fast."

He began to direct his people into the nearby houses, which proved to be deserted. The wheeled platform and the corpses of the whites, stripped of their guns and, for some mysterious reason, their hoods, were left behind.

The youth led us through the back yards of the houses, darting from building to building until he came to one he recognized. This he entered, leading us into the cellars and there pausing for breath.

"We'll leave those who're too sick to go any further here," he said. "Also the kids." He grinned at me. "What about you, mister? You can give us that rifle and go free, if you want to. There were no witnesses. You'll be all right. They'll never know there was a white man involved."

"I think that they should know," I found myself saying. "My name's Bastable. I was until recently an observer attached to General Hood's staff. I deserted and came over to the white cause. Now I have decided to serve only the cause of humanity. I am with you, Mr.—"

"Call me Paul, Mr. Bastable. Well, that was a fine speech, sir, if, might I say, a little on the prudish side! But you've proved yourself. You've got grit and grit's what's needed in these troubled times. Let's go."

He pulled back a couple of packing-cases and revealed a hole in the wall. Into this hole, which proved to give access to a passage connecting a whole series of houses, he led us, speaking to me over his shoulder as we went. "Have they started filling the cages, yet, do you know?"

"I know nothing of the cages," I told him. "I was wondering what function they were to serve. Somebody said they were Washington's 'secret weapon' against General Hood, but that mystified me even more."

"Well, it might work," said Paul, "though I'm sure most of our people would rather die."

"But what will they put in the cages? Wild beasts?"

Paul darted me an amused look. "Some would call them that, mister. They're going to put *us* in them. If Hood starts to bombard the walls, then he kills the people he intends to save. He can't liberate Washington without killing every Negro man, woman and child in the city!"

If I had been disgusted with the whites up to now, I was stunned completely by this information. It was reminiscent of the most barbaric practices I had read about in history. How could the whites regard themselves as being superior to Hood when they were prepared to use methods against him which even he had never contemplated, no matter how strong his hatred of the Caucasian race?

Washington was to be protected by a wall of living flesh!

"But all they can achieve by that is to stalemate Hood," I said. "Unless they threaten to kill your people in the hope of forcing Hood to withdraw."

"They'll do that, too, I suppose," Paul told me. We were squeezing through a very narrow tunnel now, and I heard the distant sound of rushing water. "But they've had news from the Austrajaps. If they can hold Washington for twenty-four hours, there'll be a land fleet coming to relieve them. Even those big ships of Hood's we've heard about won't be able to fire without killing their own people. Hood will have to make a decision—and either way he stands to lose something."

"They are fiends," I said. "It is impossible to regard them as human beings at all."

"I was one of Hood's special agents before I was captured," Paul said. "I was hoping to work out a way of helping him from inside, but then they rounded up every black in the city. Our only chance now is somehow to get into the main compound tonight, arm as many people as possible and try for a break."

"Do you think you'll be successful?" I asked.

Paul shook his head. "No, mister, I don't. But a lot of dead niggers won't be much use to them when Hood does come, will they?"

My nose was assailed by a sickening stench and now I realized where the sound of water had been coming from—the sewers. We were forced to wade sometimes waist-deep through foul water, emerging at last in a large underground room already occupied by about a score of Negroes. These were all that remained of those who had planned to rise in support of Hood when the moment came. They had a fair-sized arsenal with them, but it was plain that there was very little they could do now except die bravely.

Through that day we discussed our plans and, when evening came, we crept up to the surface and moved through unlit streets to the north side of the city, where the main slave compound was situated.

By the light of flares, many Negroes were still working, and it was obvious from what we heard that Hood's forces were almost here.

Our rifles on our shoulders, we marched openly along the broad streets, heading north. Anyone who saw us would have taken us for a detachment of soldiers, singularly well-disciplined. And not once were we stopped.

This had been the reason why the dead whites had been stripped of their hoods earlier that day and why, now, every man and woman in our party, with the exception of myself, wore a pair of gloves. The morbid insanity of the whites was being used against them for the first time. The hoods which they wore as a symbol of their fear and hatred of the black race were now helping members of that race to march, unchallenged, under their very noses.

Behind us, wearing fetters which could easily be removed when the moment came, were the rest of our party, dragging a big cart apparently filled with bricks but actually containing the rest of our guns.

More than once we felt we were near to discovery, but at last we reached the gates of the compound. My own accent would have been detected at once, so Paul spoke for us. He sounded most authoritative.

"Deliverin' these niggers an' pickin' up a new party," he said to the guards.

The white-hooded guards were unsuspicious. Too many were

coming and going tonight and there was more confusion than usual.

"Why are you all goin' in?" one asked as we walked through.

"Ain't you heard?" Paul told him. "There's been an outbreak. Ten or twenty of our men killed by coons."

"I heard something," another guard agreed, but by now we were inside the compound itself. It was unroofed—merely a large area in which the black slaves slept in their chains until they were required to work. A huge tub of swill in the centre of the compound was the only food. Those strong enough to crawl to the tub ate, those who were too weak either relied on their friends or starved. It did not matter to the whites, for the blacks had almost fulfilled their function, now.

We moved into the darkest part of the compound, shouting orders for the people to get to their feet and be inspected. Surreptitiously we began to hand out the weapons.

But by now we had attracted the curiosity of two of the guards, who began, casually, to walk towards us.

For my sins, I must admit that I fired the first shot. I did it without compunction, killing the guard instantly with a bullet to his heart. The others began firing, running back towards the gate, but now our luck had changed completely. Alerted by the shots, an old-fashioned steam traction-engine, crudely armoured and carrying a couple of gatlings, turned towards the compound and had filled the gate before we could reach it.

There was a pause while the occupants of this primitive land 'clad hesitated, seeing our white hoods, but the remaining guards shouted up to them to open fire.

Soon we were diving for the shadows—our only cover—as a stream of bullets raked the compound, killing with complete lack of discrimination. Many of those who were still chained were cut down where they lay and we were forced to use their bodies for cover, shooting desperately back while some of our party ran around the walls of the compound, searching for a means of escape.

But the walls were high. They had been designed so as to be escape-proof. We were trapped like rats and all we could do now was to go down fighting.

Slowly the traction-engine rolled into the compound, firing as it came. Our own bullets were useless against the armour, hastily made as it was.

Paul, who lay next to me, put a hand on my arm. "Well, Mr. Bastable, you can console yourself that you picked the right side before you died."

"It's not much comfort," I said.

Then the ground just in front of us suddenly heaved up, rippling like the waves of the sea, and something metallic and familiar emerged, its spiral snout spinning with an angry whine, directly in the path of the traction-engine. The sound of the gatlings stopped and was replaced by the dull *boom boom* of an electric cannon.

Now two more metal "moles" broke the surface, also firing. Within seconds the traction-engine was reduced to a pile of twisted wreckage and the moles moved forward, still firing, blasting great holes in the walls of the compound.

I think we were cheering as we followed behind those strange machines. I am sure that O'Bean had never visualized such a use for them! Every white hood we saw (we were no longer wearing our own) was a target and we shot at it.

I suppose it had been naïve of me to think that so clever a strategist as General Hood would not have taken the trouble to learn what the defenders of Washington had planned—and taken steps to counter their scheme. We spread out from the compound, heading for the park spaces where there were still some bushes to give us cover.

And now I heard a distant noise, reminding me more than anything else of the sound a carpet makes when it is being beaten. But I knew what the noise signified.

Seconds later explosive shells began to whistle down upon Washington.

The Land Leviathan was coming.

We regrouped as best we could, using the armed digging machines for cover, but keeping in the open as much as possible. Throughout the city now there were growing spots of light as buildings were fired by the Land Leviathan's incendiary shells.

My own view of the Battle of Washington was an extremely partial one, for I witnessed nothing of the strategy. Hood had heard that A.J.F. reinforcements were on their way and had moved his army swiftly, planning to strike and overwhelm the city well before its allies could arrive. Moreover, he knew that he would not be expected to attack at night, but it was immaterial to him at what hour he moved, for the lights of the Land Leviathan could pick out a target at almost any range.

As we fought our own little hit-and-run battle through the streets, I saw the great beams from the monster's searchlights dart out from the blackness, touch a building, marking it for destruction. Immediately would come that thunderous booming followed by a shrill whine and then an explosion as the shells struck home.

Not that Washington was helpless. Her own guns, particularly those in the Capitol itself, kept up a constant return fire and I think the ordinary land ironclads of the Black Horde would have had little chance of taking the city on their own.

Somehow I became separated from the rest of my party when a shell burst nearby and caused us to scatter. When the smoke cleared, the steel "moles" had moved on, the little army of former slaves going with them. I felt isolated and extremely vulnerable then and began to search for my comrades, but twice had to change direction as a party of white-hooded soldiers spotted me and began firing.

For an hour I kept low, sniping at the enemy when I saw him, then darting away again. My instinct was to make for a building and climb to the roof where I would be able to see the whites without being seen myself, but I knew that it would be foolish to attempt such a thing now, for buildings were being smashed to pieces all around me, under the steady bombardment of the Land Leviathan's many cannon.

I slowly made my way back towards the centre and found that most of the enemy soldiers had been ordered to the walls. Suddenly there was relative peace near the Capitol, save for the booming of the guns situated inside the building. I sat down behind a bush to collect my thoughts and get my bearings, when I heard the sound of horses' hoofs clattering towards me. They were coming very fast. I peered from behind my bush and was astonished to see a large number of horsemen streaming hell-for-leather away from the walls, as if the Devil himself was after them. The riders had removed their hoods and their faces were grim and frightened and they shouted at their mounts to give them more speed. Behind them, in a light, open carriage, came 'President' Beesley, yelling wildly. Then came the running men. Many had abandoned their weapons and had evidently panicked. I lay in my cover, but need not have feared these soldiers. They were far too terrified to stop and deal with me.

I next became aware of the ground trembling beneath me. Had God finally made up His mind to act, to punish us all for what we were doing? Had He sent an earthquake to destroy Washington?

A rumbling grew, louder and louder, and I peered ahead of me into the darkness as I gradually began to realize what was happening.

Lights blazed from the night. Lights which had their

source high overhead, so that they might have been the lights of airships. But they were not the lights of airships—all Hood's aerial battleships, it later emerged, being concentrated on harassing the Australasian-Japanese land fleet even now on its way to Washington. They were the glaring "eyes" of the Land Leviathan itself.

On it came, breaking down everything which stood in its wake, cutting a swathe through buildings, gun-emplacements, monuments. The air was filled with a ghastly, grinding sound, the snorting of the exhaust from its twelve huge engines, the peculiar sighing it gave out whenever its wheels turned it in a slightly new direction.

This vast, moving ziggurat of destruction was what had panicked Beesley and his men. It had first pounded the city with its guns and then moved forward, breaking through the walls where they were thought to be the strongest. Invincible, implacable, it rolled towards the Capitol.

Now it was my turn to take to my heels, barely managing to fling myself clear as it advanced, sighed again, and then stopped, looking up at the Capitol in what seemed to me an attitude of challenge.

Almost hysterically, the Capitol's guns swung round and began firing and I had the impression, even as I risked death to watch, that I witnessed two primitive beasts from the Earth's remote past in conflict.

The shells from the Capitol scored direct hit upon direct hit, but they merely burst against the turrets of the Land Leviathan which did not at first reply.

Then the two top turrets began to turn until almost all her guns were pointed directly at the great, white dome which even now reflected the flames of the buildings which burned all around it.

Twice the guns of the Land Leviathan spoke, in rapid

succession. The first barrage took the entire roof away. The second demolished the walls and the Capitol was silent. Again, the vast metal monster began to lumber forward, its searchlights roaming this way and that as if seeking out any others who might wish to challenge it.

At last the Land Leviathan rolled up and over the smoking, burning ruins while the air still resounded with the screams of those who had not been killed outright, who had been crushed beneath its great wheels or trapped somewhere under its belly. It rolled to the centre of the ruins and it stopped, squatting on the bones of its prey. Then, one by one, its lights began to wink out as the dawn rose behind it.

Now, indeed, the Land Leviathan was a triumphant beast.

CHAPTER FIVE
A Matter of Loyalties

Ironically enough, it had been Mrs. Persson who had commanded the group of metal "moles" which had saved us in the compound. As I stood staring up at the Land Leviathan, oblivious of all else, I heard a shout from behind me, and there she was, her body half out of the forward hatch, waving to me.

"Good morning, Mr. Bastable. I thought we had lost you."

I turned towards her, feeling very tired now. "Is it over?"

"Very nearly. We've received wireless reports that the Australasian-Japanese fleet has once again turned tail. It heard, over its own apparatus, that Washington was ours. I think they will be willing to negotiate the terms of a treaty with us now. Within the week we shall be heading South. The month should see the whole United States liberated."

For once I did not respond sardonically to that word. Having witnessed the ferocity of the whites, I truly believed that the blacks had been liberated.

"Thank you for saving my life," I said.

She smiled and made a little bow. "It was time I repaid you

for what you did for me." She looked up at a clear, cold sky. "Do you think it will snow, Mr. Bastable?"

I shrugged and trudged towards the metal mole. "Can you give me a lift, Mrs. Persson?"

"Willingly, Mr. Bastable."

W ell, Moorcock, that is pretty much the end of the tale I had for you. I remained in Hood's service for the whole of the first year he spent in the United States. There was some pretty bloody fighting, particularly, as we had expected, in parts of the South (though there were also some areas where we discovered whites and blacks living in perfect harmony!) and not all of Hood's methods of warfare were pleasant. On the other hand he was never unjust in his dealings with the defeated and never matched the ferocity and brutality of those we had encountered in Washington. Hood was not a kindly conqueror and he had the blood of many on his hands, but he was, in his own way, a just one. I was reminded, originally against my will, of William the Conqueror and the stern fair-mindedness with which he set about the pacification of England in the eleventh century.

Among other things, I had witnessed the public hanging of 'President' Beesley (discovered in the very sewers the blacks had used when hiding from him!) and many of his senior supporters, including 'Bomber' Joe Kennedy. That had not been pretty, particularly since Beesley and several of the others had died in a manner that was by no means manly.

Yet no sooner had Hood established his power than he set his war-machines to peaceful purposes. Huge ploughs were adapted, to be drawn by the ironclads, which could make a whole field ready for planting in a matter of minutes. The airships carried supplies wherever they were needed and only the Land Leviathan was not used. It remained where it had been since the morning after the battle, a symbol of Hood's triumph. Later, the monster *would* be used when required, but Hood thought it politic to leave it where it was for a while, and I suppose he was right.

In the meantime, negotiations took place with the Australasian-Japanese Federation and a truce was agreed upon. Privately, Hood thought that it might be a temporary truce and that, having once broken their policy of isolationism, the Australasian-Japanese might attempt, at some future date, to invade. It was another reason why, during the talks which took place in Washington, he left the Land Leviathan in its position, glowering down upon us while we bargained. My own feelings were not entirely in accord with his. I thought it best to show them that we were no threat to their security, for after all they still had O'Bean working for them, but Hood said that there would be time enough in the future to show good faith; now we must not let them believe they could strike again while we were off-guard. President Gandhi would not have approved, but eventually I gave in to his logic.

I made one visit to Bantustan during the course of that year, to arrange for food and medical supplies to be sent out, for it would be some time before America was entirely self-supporting. It was a peculiar alliance, that between Gandhi, the man of peace, and Hood, the Black Attila, the quintessential warlord, but it seemed to be an alliance which would work, for both men had great respect for each other. During my leisure moments, I penned this 'memoir'—mainly for your eyes, Moorcock, because I feel that I owe you something. If you can publish it—if you ever see it— well and good. Pretend that it is fiction.

I spent a considerable amount of time in the company of Mrs. Persson. She continued to remain a mysterious figure. I attempted to engage her in conversation about my previous adventures in a future age and she listened politely to me, but refused to be drawn. However, rightly or wrongly, I conceived the impression that she, like me, had also traveled through time and in various 'alternate' worlds. I also felt that she could so travel at will and I desperately hope that one day she will admit this and help me in returning to my own world. As it is, I have given her this manuscript and told her about you, the Valley of the Morning, and how important it is to me that you should read it. The rest I have left to her. It is quite possible that my convictions about her are wholly erroneous, but I think not. I even wonder how much she was responsible for Hood's successes.

Black America is now a full partner in the Ashanti Empire. Her wealth returns and Negroes are running the country. The remaining whites are in menial positions, generally speaking, and will remain so for some time. Hood told me that he intends "to punish one generation for the crimes of its forefathers". As the older generation dies out, according to Hood's plan, he will gradually lift his heel from the neck of the white race. I suppose that it *is* justice, of a sort, though I cannot find it in my heart to approve wholly.

Myself and Una Persson, of course, are hated by the majority of whites in America. We are regarded as traitors and worse. But Mrs. Persson seems thoroughly unmoved by their opinion and I am only embarrassed by it.

However, I am a creature of my own age, and a year was about the most I could take of Hood's America. Many of his men were good enough to tell me that they did not think of me as white at all, but got on with me as easily as any black man. I appreciated what they meant, but it by no means made up for the thinly disguised distaste with which I was regarded by many of the people with whom I had to mix at Hood's 'court'. Thus, eventually, I begged the Black Attila's permission to rejoin the service of Bantustan. Tomorrow I shall board an airship which will take me back to Cape Town. Once there I'll decide what to do.

You'll remember I speculated on my fate once—wondering if I was doomed to wander through a variety of different ages, of worlds slightly different from my own, to experience the many ways in which Man can destroy himself or rebuild himself into something better. Well, I still wonder that, but I have the feeling that I do not enjoy the rôle. One day, I'll probably go back to Teku Benga and enter that passage again, hope that it will take me through to a world where I am known, where my relatives will recognize me and I them, where the good old British Empire continues on its placid, decent course and the threat of a major war is very remote indeed. It's not much to hope for, Moorcock, is it?

And yet, just as I feel a peculiar loyalty to you to try to get this story to you somehow, so I am beginning to develop a loyalty not to one man, like Hood or even Gandhi, not to one nation, one world or even one period of history! My loyalty is at once to myself and to all mankind. It's hard for me to explain, for I'm not a thinking man, and I suppose it looks pretty silly written down, but I hope you'll understand.

I don't suppose, Moorcock, that I shall ever see you again, but you never know. I could turn up on your doorstep one day, with another 'tall tale' to tell you. But if I do turn up, then perhaps you should start worrying, for it could mean a war!

Good luck, old man.

Yours,
Oswald Bastable

EPILOGUE

It was getting on towards evening by the time I read the last few pages of Bastable's manuscript, then picked up his note again, plainly written some time later, when he had become more depressed:

I am going to try my luck again. This time if I am not successful I doubt I shall have the courage to continue with my life (if it *is* mine).

I sighed, turning the note over and over in my hand, baffled and feeling that I must surely, this time, be dreaming.

Una Persson had gone—vanished into nowhere with her bandits and her guns of peculiar design and unbelievable efficiency (surely proof of Bastable's own story and of his theories concerning her!). All I had left was the horse which, if I was lucky, if I did not lose my bearings, if I wasn't slaughtered by bandits, might get me back, say, to Shanghai. I had lost most of my baggage, a fair amount of money and a good deal of time, and all I had to show for it was a mystifying manuscript! Moreover, Una Persson herself had become just as tantalizing a mystery as Bastable. I was very little better off, as regards my own peace of mind, than when I set out.

Eventually I rose, went to my own room, and fell immediately asleep. In the morning I felt almost surprised when I saw the manuscript still beside me and, as I peered from my window, the horse placidly cropping at some sparse grass. I found a piece of paper and scribbled a note to Mrs. Persson, thanking her for her hospitality and her manuscript. Then, by way of a joke that was half serious, I scribbled my address in London and invited her to drop in and see me "if you are ever in my part of the twentieth century again".

A month later, thin and exhausted, I arrived in Shanghai. I spent no more time in China than was necessary to get a passage home.

And here, sitting at my desk in my little study with its window overlooking the rolling, permanent hills of the West Riding, I read through Bastable's manuscript and I try to understand the implications of his adventures, and I fail.

If anyone else *ever* reads this, perhaps they will be able to make more of it than I.

EDITOR'S NOTE

Bastable was mystified, my grandfather was mystified, and I must confess to being mystified myself—though such speculations are supposed to be my stock-in-trade. I have used, quite shamelessly, in novels of my own, some of the ideas found in the book I've named *The Warlord of the Air*, and, indeed, one or two of the characters (specifically Una Persson, who appears in *The English Assassin*) have been 'lifted'. Perhaps Mrs. Persson will some time come across one of these books. If she does, I very much hope she will pay me a visit—and possibly give me an answer to the mystery of Oswald Bastable. I assure you that the moment she does, I shall pass the news on!

MICHAEL MOORCOCK

Somewhere in the twentieth century

ABOUT THE AUTHOR

Michael Moorcock is a prolific and award-winning writer with more than eighty works of fiction and non-fiction to his name. He is the creator of Elric of Melniboné, the Eternal Champion Jerry Cornelius and Colonel Pyat, amongst many other memorable characters. He is also the author of the *Hawksmoon* series of science-fantasy novels and the original *Doctor Who* novel, *The Coming of the Terraphiles*. Born in London, Moorcock now divides his time between Paris, France and Austin, Texas.

www.multiverse.org

PHILIP JOSÉ FARMER

Brand-new editions of classic novels from one of the greatest science-fiction writers of the 20th century. Each novel containing unique bonus material from well-known Farmer experts and fans.

WOLD NEWTON SERIES

The Other Log of Phileas Fogg
Time's Last Gift
Wold Newton Short Story Collection (October 2013)
(Prehistory)
Time's Last Gift
Hadon of Ancient Opar
(Parallel Universe)
A Feast Unknown
Lord of the Trees
The Mad Goblin (June 2013)

GRANDMASTER SERIES

Lord Tyger
The Wind Whales of Ishmael
Flesh (August 2013)
Venus on the Half-Shell (December 2013)